UNDER PRESSURE

NewCon Press Novellas

Set 1: Science Fiction (Cover art by Chris Moore)
The Iron Tactician – Alastair Reynolds
At the Speed of Light – Simon Morden
The Enclave – Anne Charnock
The Memoirist – Neil Williamson

Set 2: Dark Thrillers (Cover art by Vincent Sammy)
Sherlock Holmes: Case of the Bedevilled Poet – Simon Clark
Cottingley – Alison Littlewood
The Body in the Woods – Sarah Lotz
The Wind – Jay Caselberg

Set 3: The Martian Quartet (Cover art by Jim Burns)
The Martian Job – Jaine Fenn
Sherlock Holmes: The Martian Simulacra – Eric Brown
Phosphorous: A Winterstrike Story – Liz Williams
The Greatest Story Ever Told – Una McCormack

Set 4: Strange Tales (Cover art by Ben Baldwin)
Ghost Frequencies – Gary Gibson
The Lake Boy – Adam Roberts
Matryoshka – Ricardo Pinto
The Land of Somewhere Safe – Hal Duncan

Set 5: The Alien Among Us (Cover art by Peter Hollinghurst)
Nomads – Dave Hutchinson
Morpho – Philip Palmer
The Man Who Would be Kling – Adam Roberts
Macsen Against the Jugger – Simon Morden

Set 6: Blood and Blade (Cover art by Duncan Kay)
The Bone Shaker – Edward Cox
A Hazardous Engagement – Gaie Sebold
Serpent Rose – Kari Sperring
Chivalry – Gavin Smith

Set 7: Robot Dreams (Cover art by Fangorn)
According To Kovac – Andrew Bannister
Deep Learning – Ren Warom
Paper Hearts – Justina Robson
The Beasts Of Lake Oph – Tom Toner

UNDER PRESSURE

Fabio Fernandes

NewCon Press
England

First published in the UK by NewCon Press
41 Wheatsheaf Road, Alconbury Weston, Cambs, PE28 4LF
September 2022

NCP285 (limited edition hardback)
NCP286 (softback)

10 9 8 7 6 5 4 3 2 1

ISBN:

978-1-914953-30-9 (hardback)
978-1-914953-31-6 (softback)

Cover art and front cover graphics by Justin Tan
Back cover layout by Ian Whates

Editorial meddling by Ian Whates
Typesetting by Ian Whates

For Michael Moorcock and Roger Zelazny

ONE

"In essence, there are three kinds of dreams. The most common kind is what we call the normal dream, full of imagery from memory and the unconscious thought. In this type of dream, the dreamer does not know he is dreaming. Every being in all known realities is capable of having such dreams. The second variety is the lucid dream, where things feel more concrete and coherent. In this kind of dream, the dreamer knows he is dreaming, and in some cases he can wake spontaneously at will. Most of human beings across the universes can have such dreams. The third type is accessible only by a handful of people; it is the kind of dream that requires not only that the dreamer is conscious, but also that he knows he is entering a neutral dimension (the Existing) and from there he may, at his will, enter different realities, which are not dreams, but existing worlds. This particular kind of dreamer is an Oneironaut, or dream-traveller."

– From *In Libro Somnium*

Less than a week before the Martian Invasion, January Purcell was on her way to Camden when the sky fell again.

She never got used to the feeling of having a brick wall toppling down with full force on her head. But that couldn't be helped. The good thing was that she was alone in a hansom cab, and nobody saw her hitting her head on the cabin's back panel and nearly fainting with the pain that seemed to come from inside her brain.

Incoming memories was all she could think, recognising the sensation. She closed her eyes and took a deep breath, letting her pulse slow back down and entering a meditation trance. It would take her quite some time to absorb all the information she had just received from her counterpart in another reality.

Time she no longer had. The cab stopped right in front of her destination.

The substantial house at 77 Great Russell Street was once occupied by architect Thomas Henry Wyatt, who designed houses, rectories and hospitals; and churches, lots of churches. But this house wasn't one of his projects, sadly.

It was a fine construction, all the same. She knew that Shelley had lived somewhere on that same street. Where, exactly? Alas, she didn't have time to find out. January climbed the small flight of stairs and knocked on the door.

She introduced herself to the governess, a short, stocky old lady with a pinched face, and was immediately ushered into the scriptorium, where her employer waited.

Dr. Jones was an impressive man in all aspects: a very tall, thin, pallid man, with ash blond hair neatly cut and combed, he was sitting in a wingback chair by the fire. He was dressed rather formally, as if for a soirée. The emerald silk puff tie matched the impressive – and very bold – viridian suit. The burnished gold waistcoat matched his hair.

In his well-manicured, blue-veined white hands, the impeccably dressed scientist held a book with red-leather cover and lettering richly embossed in gold: *Vedanta Philosophy*, by Swami Vivekananda.

"Please, Miss Purcell, do take a seat." He gestured to another, identical chair in front of him. He waved the book gently, almost timidly: "Don't think less of me on account of my readings. I can assure you every single thing I read has a purpose."

January sat, smiling. "I would never think less of you, Dr. Jones. On the contrary: I'm an admirer of your work."

"And how do you know my work?" He seemed genuinely curious.

She evaded the question for the time being. "Your name is quite well known in the right circles." He wasn't that famous yet, and she had to be very careful with what information she could disclose. "I've heard that you were in search of assistants for an important project. Here I am."

He looked at her intently. Putting his book aside, he crossed his legs – long legs, long and thin as a spider's – and steepled his fingers. "In what capacity?"

"I studied Geology under Professor Charles Lyell." And, before he could say anything, she added: "Since Professor Lyell is no longer with us, I must say that I also have a degree from Oxford, which I am more than happy to produce in case you require proof."

He shook his head. "No, my dear, that won't be necessary. I'm far more interested in the practical applications of science. Diplomas are not that important."

"I'm willing and able to assist you with experiments and any sort of scientific work."

"Brilliant!" he exclaimed. And then, suddenly: "Why do people wage wars, Miss Purcell?"

She was intrigued by the question, but was expecting it somehow, so she promptly retorted: "Not people, Dr. Jones. Nations."

"Exactly," he said, apparently pleased by her line of reasoning. "Nations fight wars, not people. They do so to remain the way they are. They occupy territories, they enslave people, they command resources at their pleasure. And these resources are what make nations, essentially. If you have more of a given resource, of something which other nations are desperately in need, then you are a rich nation."

"But it depends of what kind of resource we are talking about. The British are very poor on agriculture, for one thing."

"Yes. On the other hand, we are exceedingly good in warfare," he said, a bit sombre. "Weapons allowed us to become an Empire."

"Such is the colonial mentality."

He smiled. "I see you agree with me, Miss Purcell."

"I wouldn't expect our conversation to be different, Dr. Jones."

"Do you know what the Vedanta is?"

She shook her head, lying in gesture if not with words. She had her share of contact with Eastern systems of thought, but it was important to hear what he had to say. She needed to gather information about him.

"To sum it up very poorly, this Indian philosophy teaches us many things, not least among which is the fact that service for humanity is a service for oneself. That is, man should help his fellow men, not hinder them under any fallacy such as superiority of race, sex, and finance."

"I see we really do agree with each other, Dr. Jones."

He leaned forward.

"Do you see this eye, Miss Purcell?"

Indeed she saw it. His right eye was brown – she couldn't fail to notice that his left one was blue, but that wasn't the only difference between them. The pupil of Dr. Jones's right eye seemed permanently dilated.

"I was attacked by a thug in Afghanistan," he said. "Ghastly business. He was only a lad. A lad insane, I'm afraid. I almost lost it. I can barely see with it, but that's of no consequence. I bear no ill will towards the lad. In fact, I can't blame him. I do blame, however, politics. If we had minded our own business and left them to theirs, nothing of the sort would have happened. Since my return to England, I have been searching for means of making the world better, and one of my many endeavours is related to researching new, efficient sources of energy. Coal is our greatest enemy today, Miss Purcell. The mining alone is responsible for ending thousands of lives prematurely. Not to mention this dreadful fog that causes so many diseases. A true scientist cannot attribute these dreadful emissions merely to miasmas."

January nodded in agreement. "Indeed he can't, Dr. Jones. Am I to suppose that you have discovered a new source, then?"

"I might have, Miss Purcell. Would you be so kind as to return here tomorrow morning? I will gather the other brains and arms I collected to this enterprise. Please be here at ten o'clock sharp." He stood up. "Now, if you'll excuse me, I have other business to attend. Something unexpected has come up. Do you need a ride?"

"No, Dr. Jones, thank you. It's a fine evening. I'd rather walk home."

TWO

"Every being has a counterpart in all the known realities. The focus here is on humans, more specifically Oneironauts, but it is safe to assume that even animals have counterparts. Usually there is no recollection, no unbroken stream of consciousness between realities, so one person is alone with his own thoughts at any given moment in any particular reality. However, every time an Oneironaut cross over, he retains the memories of his previous 'incarnation', so to speak, for the duration of his mission. It is not clear if this is a natural process or something concocted by the Higher Order."

— From *The Book of Oneiric Rules*

January's lodgings in Marylebone were quite a long walk from Great Russell Street, but she decided to return home by foot all the same, to better ponder what she had just experienced. She walked as slowly as she could, soaking up the newly imprinted images, sounds, and thoughts of her counterpart as if her brain were a sponge.

When she entered her small, modest apartment on Marylebone Road, she had everything pretty much sorted out. She picked the kettle to boil water for the tea and sat back in her favourite chair, a Windsor model all in black, to think.

This Doctor Jones seemed to be an interesting man, but her counterpart had already implied that. At least in terms of Jones' own counterpart in that other reality. But she was quite confident he was indeed a remarkable man by her own account: during their brief interview, January conducted a quick browse of the shelves in his scriptorium. A small but brilliant library: January could recall titles by Verne and Wells. Also Shaw, Wilde, Bellamy. The regular stuff, actually. But the intriguing thing had been the rest of the books surrounding the fables, plays, *voyages extraordinaires*, and scientific romances: books on engineering, mechanics, physics, and medicine. Speleology, meteorology, and cartography as well, not to mention a couple of books on Buddhism and Hinduism. Dr. Robert Jones appeared to be a polymath of the highest order. But then, she thought with a smile, all members of the Fellowship were polymaths.

A curious thing, his eyes were. Maybe his intense stare was an unexpected effect of the accident? Even so, there was no doubt in her mind that Jones knew very well how to put his handicap to good use, because his eye was exactly what he told her it was. A natural eye, if a little damaged. Not a mechanical substitute, not an offworld device.

But the signs scattered across the room were clear: he was one of them. He was an Oneironaut, even if he didn't know that yet. And he should be protected at all costs. Such was the nature of the Long Game.

The Long Game is an extension of the Great Game: while the latter is concerned with keeping the colonies of the Empire appeased and also fending off any advances of Russians, Ottomans and other rival empires, the Long Game is focused on another, more complex aspect.

Time and its malcontents.

Time travel was discovered more than a century before. It was something more akin to old narratives like Lucian of Samosata's *A True Story* or modern books like *Looking Backward* than to Wells' *The Time Machine*. Nobody can travel using machines. The only way to do it is via dreaming.

Dreams make you jump across realities so you can – sort of – become another person. Not quite another person, but your counterpart in an alternative timeline. Meaning that you simply become yourself on another world, the version of yourself you were meant to be there.

It is not an easy thing to do: first, the student of this art (called an *Oneironaut*) must undergo rigorous training in order to manipulate the dreamstate, or rather, to know its waves in order to better ride them to the planned destination. It takes time and patience.

Sanity is also a prerequisite. To be in control of one's mental faculties is important, because in order to travel into dreams the Oneironaut must know not, as you might think, the difference between dream and reality, but precisely the fact that there is *no difference* between dream and reality. A dream is just another reality, one of many, one of infinite realities some call the multiverse. The Fellowship call it officially the Oneiroverse. To its members they are of no consequence, these nomenclatures: the important thing is that it exists. But not everyone can travel by these means. The ones who can are drafted to be agents of the Long Game.

Which is not by any means confined to the British Empire in the 1800s. The Game stretches in time and into other universes. As January knows well.

She is a very experienced agent, having covered a great variety of situations in a huge swath of incredibly dissimilar universes. In some of them, January was male. In others, female. But they were always agents on service of the Fellowship. And the Fellowship needed them.

This particular case was not only related to the Great and Long Game, but also to the end of the world. Possibly the end of many worlds.

January's mission, however, wasn't an easy one. Not just because of the inherent difficulty, but also because she hadn't been properly briefed.

That happened because she was assigned to the case while she was dying.

Oneironauts are usually called to action upon sleeping, but not always. They might be reached during their waking periods by other agents, who show them a sign of their office so recognition may be established, and then deliver the assignment. Sometimes, however, things happen along the way.

During an especially complicated mission, the agent (who, in that particular reality, had a different name, but with the same initials, so let's call her/him/they JP instead) was shot twice in the midsection. They were rapidly taken to the nearest hospital, but even with the best medical technology available in 1968 (for dream-travelling is travel in time as well as in space), it wasn't easy. They had to be put into a coma.

Dreams in deep sleep are the hardest to control. The dreamer can't return until they wake up.

That's how January was pretty much conscripted to this mission.

13

When Oneironauts plan to travel, they always prepare first. Most of them perform autogenic training, which is essentially a technique of desensitisation and relaxation. But other ways are used: meditation, reading a list of objectives, even prayer, if it suits the agents' fancy. There is no particular method written in stone. The only condition is that the Oneironaut use something that helps keep in mind the path to the final destination.

January likes to write.

Virtually all their counterparts do it. Almost always in paper notebooks, although some use electronic devices (when available) outside or inside the body. As for her, the weapon of choice is the pen. She writes anything she thinks relevant. For instance, the contents of the last time she dreamtravelled in a planned fashion were:

- Timetables of trains between Bath and London during the Blitz;
- Trusted apothecaries in Amsterdam where certain kinds of poisons could be bought without prescription in the late seventeenth century;
- Rhyming slang in Birmingham around 1957;
- Currency in same area;
- Where to find a good old books shop;
- Where to find a restaurant with decent food (no fish and chips, no steak and kidney pie or curry acceptable) in Bournemouth in 1982.

That, however, was not to be the case when JP was admitted to hospital and had an emergency surgery. They went quickly under anesthesia, which in 1968 was already powerful enough to take you under for a long time, and started the voyage.

JP felt the wisps of sleep starting to come off slowly, as if they were inside a bleak house full of cobwebs. Very thick cobwebs. They proceeded to tear them apart so they could pass through the many narrow undefined rooms, searching for the light at the end of it. And eventually they saw it.

Even when the journey is impromptu, a trained Oneironaut is capable of seeing the new reality clearly, though they might not always have chosen it. That was true in JP's case. There was only one pinprick of light ahead of them, not several, as usually is the case. There are endless rooms in the House.

So, having seen the light at the end of the trail, JP approached it – and what they saw was peril.

Sometimes, the Oneironaut is drawn to a situation of clear and present danger. At such times there is nothing for them to do but submit, to let themselves go with the flow, and arrive safely, despite the unsafe environment.

Fortunately, JP still managed to navigate through the reefs of dream, and reached their destination.

It wasn't hard to understand where they were. The buildings around her were all too familiar: they were still in London.

As to the when, it wasn't that hard either. Judging by the clothes of the people in the street and the vehicles, all of them horse-drawn, they were in the second half of the nineteenth century. The eighties or nineties, most probably. It was only when JP approached a newsboy to buy a paper that the *who* became clear.

They reached for the trouser pockets to pick a coin to pay the boy, but the hand slid over fabric that most definitely didn't feel like wool. It was a dress.

Not quite a dress, actually; more a topcoat and a skirt, with a small rear pad to enhance their posterior. And the mandatory, and very uncomfortable, corset. Definitely the 1880s.

So, now, they were a *she*.

January Purcell, she remembered her name then, as often happens when you exit the dreamstate fully. JP woke up to the new reality, and it was only their training that impeded them to forget their immediately previous self.

She then discovered in the folds of the dress a small purse, which she opened to find some bills and coins. She bought the paper and saw the date: May 16th, 1888.

Her birthday. Or rather, she corrected herself, the birthday of one of her counterparts.

She took a deep breath and let herself go. Since here January was a native, and not a member of the Fellowship, she would get her bearings soon enough, and so she did. In fact, when this swooning sensation took her, she happened to have just left a friend's house to visit her newborn child and have some tea. Now she was returning home – or rather, her rented apartment in the City. She had just arrived from Oxford, where she passed the last four years studying, and from where she took a train to London for an interview the following day. If everything went well, she would soon be working with several brilliant minds, on a project she didn't know much about, but which she now felt sure had everything to do with what was going to happen in approximately a week from now, namely, the end of the world.

And, though JP was by no means alone (for there was help to be found here, and she knew how), she was very much on her own. For she was the only one right now who knew the end was near. And she would have to convince her fellow Oneironauts of that reality.

As far as she could remember, the Oneiros Club had existed since the early nineteenth century. Her male counterpart was familiar with that old (by 1968's standards) bastion of conservative English reality-hoppers. They could help her get her bearings and better assess the situation. January drank her tea in silence. Time to worry about that later, after her next meeting with Dr. Jones.

THREE

Upon reaching a given reality, the Oneironaut, after acclimating himself — a process that should not take too long, for time is still of the essence any-where or any-when he finds himself — must do two things: first, he must establish his priorities, knowing what he is being called to act upon (his mission). And second, he must search for allies who can help him to further the good execution of his deeds. Unfortunately, the existence of allies does not exclude the possible existence of enemies, for whom the Oneironaut should be alert at all times.

— From the Diaries of Franz Mesmer

January was back at 77 Great Russell Street at five minutes to ten the next morning. She wasn't the first to arrive.

This time, though, she wasn't ushered to Dr. Jones's scriptorium by the governess. The role of guide was taken by a silent man with bushy black side-whiskers and a moustache, dressed in a grey tweed suit, a stiff-crowned hat in his hand. The clothes and the hat made it clear to January that he was no butler, but instead a friend or associate of Dr. Jones. He gestured for her to enter, a clumsy bow that was a crude attempt at elegance, but when he straightened up again, January had the chance to look at his eyes. The man, who was still silent, had the deepest blue eyes she had ever seen, not only in that life but in all the others she could remember. They gleamed coldly in the dimness of the hall.

She hurried in. The silent man closed the door quickly and went right to the stairs. January followed. They descended in silence to the basement, where January could see a brightly illuminated workshop. The place was filled with benches and tables, all strewn with beakers, test tube racks, and all sorts of mechanical parts of what appeared to be engines. The cellar was somewhat narrow, but long; at the other end of it, Dr. Jones was talking across a narrow table to a woman dressed entirely in black, who seemed to listen attentively. The table top was bare, with the exception of a black-lacquered box that seemed to suck in the light around it. Dr. Jones hovered over the box, protectively. The whole scene seemed bathed in a very faint, phantasmagorically bluish light, which melted into the pools of clarity of the lamps when she approached the table.

"Good morning, Miss Purcell," he said. "Please join us. Thank you, Mr. Moran, for bringing her to our meeting."

Mr. Moran — at least now January knew his name, if not his voice — only nodded. Moran approached the table from behind, standing right at Dr. Jones' side. January preferred to stay across the table from the men, siding with the woman, who she now noticed was very young. Up close, January could see that her black garments were quite sensible, almost rational: the woman wore a blouse with a corset and a short skirt, Annie Oakley-style, with a hem reaching the shins. It looked more comfortable than January's own conservative dress, she couldn't fail to observe.

"You have already met my valet, Mr. Moran," Dr. Jones said. "Now allow me to introduce Miss Marie Sklodowska. She came from Warsaw by way of Paris. She was working until very recently with Monsieur Pierre Curie, a French physicist with whom I have been corresponding, and whose recent discovery in crystallography will help us immensely."

"It's a pleasure to meet you. Pardon my English," Sklodowska said, extending her hand to shake January's in a vigorous grip. "I'm better in French."

"*Pas de problème, mademoiselle*," January said. "*Je parle Français aussi.*"

Sklodowska smiled. They would be good friends, January decided.

"So, since everybody is here now, I will explain my plan," Dr. Jones said. "One of my research subjects is the study of fuel resources. I started with coal, which is one of the most used products and also the most harmful to humans, animals and plants, for that matter. I have also been studying the use of petroleum, which has been used for a while now in America. Even electricity has not escaped my attention, though I am quite convinced it won't be efficient for at least a century.

"So, I concentrated on coal. And what is coal, I ask you?" he looked around, and January saw this wasn't a rhetorical question.

"Coal is a combustible sedimentary rock," she promptly answered. "It's mostly carbon with variable amounts of other elements; chiefly hydrogen, sulphur, oxygen, and nitrogen."

"Precisely, my dear January," Dr. Jones said very seriously. January noticed, however, that his eyes – or at least his good eye – smiled at her in a most intriguing and beautiful way. "And how is it formed?"

"Allow me to explain that one for you, Dr. Jones," Mr. Moran suddenly interrupted, to January's surprise. The man seemed more than a bit anxious, and that was already a bit too much for January's taste. She saw that Sklodowska flinched the instant he started talking. The Polish scientist was definitely bothered by his manners.

"Please do, Mr. Moran," Dr. Jones said after a couple of seconds. He didn't show any emotion, but January assumed that the pause had been deliberate, a way for him to express his discomfort. The man, who had been so silent until that moment, now couldn't wait to run his mouth off. January caught herself wondering about him. Moran was a rather common name, but she was sure she had heard it before in a significant context. Where, though?

"Coal is formed when dead plants decay into peat, basically," Moran explained. "With the passing of the ages, this substance ends up buried under the earth. Then the heat and the pressure of deep burial converts the peat into the sedimentary rock known as coal," he recited as if he was reading a text book. "This whole process started –"

"Exactly, Mr. Moran," Dr. Jones interrupted him. "*Pressure* being the keyword here. A process that takes millions of years is something not to be taken lightly. Imagine, if you please, the sheer amount of energy required to form coal. Now, let us take a leap further and imagine: what next in this geological evolutionary ladder of sorts?"

"Diamonds," said January.

"Precisely. The most coveted mineral in the world."

"Not as rare as some would like it, mind you, sir," Moran scoffed.

"Indeed, they are not rare in existence. They are, however, hard to acquire. They don't bloom on topsoil but can only be found deep inside the earth."

"I thought," Sklodowska said, "that they could be found in river beds as well."

At that, Moran grinned. He still seemed very keen on showing his knowledge. "Oh, Miss, this is but the tip of the iceberg," he said. "There were plenty of cases of alluvial deposits twenty years ago, but today you will not find diamonds on the surface."

"I'm sorry, Dr. Jones, but I fail to understand where you're heading with this," January said, if only to stop Moran's blabber.

"Diamonds, Miss Purcell, are seen purely as objects of beauty. And yet they exist in almost the same quantity as coal."

"I'm not sure if I understand what you are implying, *Docteur*," said Sklodowska. "Are you trying to create diamonds from coal? I think I can understand the logic behind your reasoning, but it would be extremely *difficile* to attempt such a feat."

Dr. Jones laughed, shaking his head.

"No, Miss Sklodowska, nothing so simplistic. As a matter of fact, I am merely following in the footsteps of your former employer, Monsieur Curie."

"Oui," she said, appearing to be a little puzzled. "I remember he talked to you extensively about piezoelectricity."

"Exactly, my dear." The electric charge that accumulates in solid materials such as crystals in response to pressure and heat. And what are diamonds?"

"Why, crystals, Dr. Jones," Mr. Moran hastened to reply. "Crystals to which a great deal of pressure has been applied."

"My reasoning, Miss Sklodowska," Dr. Jones continued, without acknowledging his valet, "is that diamond and coal are both forms of carbon and, as such, both could be used as combustible substances. We have been mining coal for centuries now, and what do we have to be proud of? Pollution and conspurcation of the atmosphere and the water. The air is thick with the gases produced by the coal-burning of the factories. The very process of mining has a detrimental effect on the waterways, defiling the rivers with sulphur and contaminating drinking water. For that reason alone, coal should have been left untouched deep under the earth many years ago. And I've yet to mention the perils for the miners in the pits, with the limited air circulation and the noxious methane…"

"I beg your pardon, Dr. Jones." It was January who interjected now, "but there is a small flaw in your rationale."

Dr. Jones cocked his head the tiniest bit and regarded January with his bad eye. She decided he probably used this particular stare to indicate disapproval, especially if someone happened to disturb his train of thought or tried to correct him.

"And what would that flaw be, Miss Purcell?"

She didn't bat an eye. "Diamonds can't burn. They can't provide the energy we need."

At that, Dr. Jones grinned broadly. A big unsettling Cheshire Cat grin.

"Oh, Miss Purcell, but they can. Now they can."

January just raised her eyebrows.

"How, pray tell?"

"We are going to use this," and he unveiled the box in the centre of the table. It was a tortoiseshell lacquer box, approximately thirty centimetres on each side, inlaid with mother-of-pearl and gold dust. Dr. Jones opened the lid.

Leaning closer, January could see inside the box what seemed to be a metallic structure holding two small diamonds, their tips facing one another, with thin leaf of metal foil between them. She thought she recognised the apparatus from a visit to a laboratory in Leeds a couple of years ago.

"This is a diamond anvil cell," January said, almost regretting saying that aloud. As far as she could remember (but she was feeling, as she spoke, that the memories of her male counterpart were fading), this device would only be invented twenty years in the future. But that, as she had already established, was a slightly different reality.

"Indeed it is, Miss Purcell," Dr. Jones smiled, but this time it was a benevolent, one might say even joyful smile. "But there is a very important distinction in this particular apparatus. This particular anvil cell uses quap as a compressible fluid. I assume you are familiar with this substance?"

"I can't say I am."

Dr. Jones tsked. "It's a substance similar to that which my good friend H.G. Wells wrote about in one of his scientific romances. You have probably heard of Cavorite…" He made a visible effort to say the word, as if it was something forbidden or cursed.

Now January nodded. She was familiar with cavorite – if only from H.G. Wells's *The First Men in the Moon*, which she also had considered fiction. But now her memories were getting more and more anchored to that particular reality, and she could remember reading something in the newspapers about a scandal involving Mr. Cavor.

"The difference from the conventional diamond anvil cell, Miss Purcell," Dr. Jones went on, "is that this device, my little wood-and-tin machine, is going to *de-compress* the diamonds."

Now January was really curious.

"Allow me to make a demonstration," he said, closing the box. He started making adjustments via a set of knobs and levers located at the side of the contraption. January could also see a small red button just below the set.

After a few minutes, Dr. Jones finished the adjustments. "The cavorite, as it was reported by Wells, is a substance that presents negative gravitational mass."

"That means something lighter than anything you could have possibly imagined, miss," Mr. Moran told January.

"I'm quite familiar with the jargon, Mr. Moran, thank you." And, to Dr. Jones, also visibly upset by the interruption. "Please continue, Doctor."

"Very well. The quap, however, is very different from that substance because it emits a benign irradiation –"

"Radiation," Sklodowska corrected him.

"Yes, radiation," Dr Jones said, visibly bothered. "I shall now point a light source into the diamond at the top, which will then channel the beam down to the bottom one. Then, the cumulative effect will magnify this beam until, with the help of the quap, it reaches high potency, condensing the light and de-compressing the diamonds, extracting practically the same amount of potential energy used through the eons to transform them into diamonds in the first place. But all that accumulated energy will be unleashed in one single instant."

"What happens to the diamonds?" asked January.

"What indeed?" he said. And he pushed the button.

January flinched in anticipation. She was certain the whole contraption would blow up in their faces, or start to melt and exude a thick black smoke or something. But her fears were unfounded: the box simply purred ever so slightly, a vibration that would have been barely perceivable if the room hadn't become so quiet. January was intrigued: the box clearly belonged to this timeline. The technology inside it, apparently not.

In five seconds the purring stopped. Dr. Jones produced a small, portable electric torch. It was a fibre tube with brass caps on both ends and a bulls-eye glass lens at the front.

"This is a brand new model of Misell torch," he explained. "It works with D-batteries, that is, dry batteries with limited capacity and, alas, not rechargeable. But now, with this new source," he connected the rear end of the torch at a small hole near the button and the knob, which January had failed to notice, "we will have free, clean, and durable energy."

Suddenly the lamp of the torch flared to life, a powerful light that would have blinded January had she been looking straight into the tube. "And this," he added, "this application of a mere few seconds, is enough to make the torch work without interruption for approximately twenty-four hours. The diamonds, Miss Purcell, as you can see..." and he opened the box, revealing a tiny black smudge on the bottom of the box, "The diamonds are entirely spent. Bigger stones, naturally, will take more time to be transformed into pure energy, but they will also give us more power."

January did her best to recover her wits, feeling a mounting sense of anger. "But how did you come by this machine?" she asked. "Did you build it?"

"It was already invented," he answered. "In my dreams."

January didn't blink, but suddenly she became much more interested. Things were getting more intelligible now.

"I have always had the strangest dreams," Jones confessed, "since childhood. Not only the mere stuff of dream or nightmare, but also vivid images of things I could not know, for I had never seen them in my life. For instance, one night, when I was very young – sixteen – I dreamed of a palace in a Far East land, in exquisite detail, such as I had never read about nor seen in pictures."

"But your parents could have showed it to you, surely," January caught herself interrupting. She was very upset now.

Dr. Jones, though, didn't seem to mind being interrupted by her. "My parents lacked the imagination necessary to impress me with tales and pictures, Miss Purcell. My imagination is mine alone. But my dreams used to tell me – indeed, they still do tell – quite another story."

"Until a year ago, these dreams plagued me. I was plagued by them incessantly, several per night, to such an extent that I used to wake up exhausted and, worse, having almost no recollection of what had transpired in those dreams. I strongly believe that not knowing the stuff of them was making me ill.

"Then I met someone who was able to help in this regard, and, in doing so, changed my life in so many other ways as well. A certain Doctor Spottiswoode was recommended by a friend. Through him I had access to a new medication, which he called Pausodyne. This medication, administered in small doses, is a capital anaesthetic. In larger doses, however, it puts the patient in a state that Dr. Spottiswoode calls 'suspended animation'. The patient lies dormant, without even the need to breathe, for long periods, such as wild beasts might do when hibernating during winter."

"And you received a larger dose, I presume?" January was more flabbergasted by the second. And yet, she had to keep her wits about her if she wanted to get to the bottom of this.

"I did, yes. It put me to sleep, or a close approximation, for three days. I woke up refreshed, and from them on I was able to dream in a more orderly fashion."

"And what would that orderly fashion be?"

"A dream per night," he said. "A long, complex dream, as real as it can possibly be. Sometimes the dream even acquires a very interesting configuration, and I find myself having the same dream

24

again for several nights, but not a repetition. More by way of continuation. As if it was a…" he searched for the metaphor, but January already had a pretty good idea of the image he would choose. "As if it was a house with many rooms, and I only visited one or two each night."

The House.

When January became an Oneironaut (a long, long time ago), she was given a map of sorts to the House. This kind of place, or non-place, as her instructors were always keen to correct her, is part of a larger thing called The Existing. This, a bigger world that encompasses all the other worlds, and of which Earth is but a shadow, is so incomprehensible to the human mind that early Oneironauts had to conjure a more suitable environment to work in. Hence the House.

The House is never the same for any two Oneironauts. January couldn't say what it looked like for others, but for her this non-place would manifest as a huge old Victorian mansion, with dozens of rooms, maybe more; no, certainly more, but she never had the whole tour, and sometimes she wondered if she would one day get to know the entire House. *Better not to dwell on such things*, she thought. *Focus*.

"Be as it may, one night I dreamt of this contraption," he went on, "but also of something else. I dreamt of an old presence."

"A presence?" January said, feeling a chill up her spine despite herself, and hoping against hope he was not referring to the Old Ones. She had met them in the past, and wished fervently that she would never meet them again.

"At first I thought it was a spirit, but then I realised it was merely an old man. Old, and wise beyond his years. We met in a tunnel under Snæfellsjökull."

"And where is that?"

"Forgive me, my dear. Oftentimes I forget not everyone is privy to the same study as I am." January winced at that blatant display of English male arrogance. "Snæfellsjökull is an extinct volcano in Iceland."

"Oh," January remembered, and then couldn't keep to herself any more. "As in Jules Verne's *Journey to the Centre of the Earth?*"

It was Dr. Jones' turn to wince.

"Not quite, Miss Purcell. As you well know, Professor Lidenbrock was a friend of Verne's. His narrative is a flight of fancy, I'm afraid. Very entertaining, but far from the truth. I've been corresponding with Professor Lidenbrock, and he told me that, although most of the writer's narrative is fruit of his brilliant imagination, the part of the story about the Icelandic alchemist Arne Saknussemm is very much true."

January breathed deeply. Not him. Not Saknussemm.

"And the old wise man would be this Arne…" she ventured.

"Saknussemm, yes. I have managed to talk extensively to him during my dreams, and he told me that, although the novel deals in fantasy, there are more things down there, paraphrasing the Bard, than are dreamt of in our philosophy."

"Did he tell you what those things were?"

"Not everything," Dr. Jones said. "I had the feeling he was hiding most of it from me, but what little he said served to pique my interest."

"Such as?"

"Diamonds, Miss Purcell. Diamonds that could power the whole planet for all eternity, and mankind would never again be slave to coal and other kinds of combustible materials that poison, air, land and sea."

January opened her mouth to ask if he was sure of what he was saying, but thought better of it. He wouldn't take the question lightly. Instead she said, in as non-committal a fashion as possible, "Are you planning to send a geologist there to find these diamonds?"

Then Dr. Jones smiled. A smile with too many teeth, like a predator's.

"No, Miss Purcell. I'm planning to go there in person to see it for myself. And to bring as many diamonds back with me and my group as possible."

"Your group being…?"

Dr. Jones looked at her with an expression of slight disappointment on his face. "Why, Miss Purcell. Mr. Moran here, Miss Sklodowska, and you."

"I'm sorry, Doctor, but there is also Hans," Moran finally managed to open his mouth again.

"Yes, of course. And Hans, who guided Professor Lidenbrock on his expedition. He will be waiting for us in Reykjavik in three days' time. My dirigible departs tomorrow at ten in the morning from Victoria Station. Bring winter apparel; I will provide all the necessary equipment to make the descent. If you don't have any questions left," and January noticed that he meant only her with that *you*, "I think we can end this meeting and prepare for the trip. Don't worry, Miss Purcell; we'll have a briefing inside the vessel upon departure. Feel free then to ask whatever questions you see fit then."

She could only nod, because suddenly it was as if a tableau had been dismantled; Sklodowska smiled at her and made straight for the stairs. Mr. Moran retreated to the shadowy background behind Dr. Jones, who proceeded to close the box with utmost care, ceasing to paying attention to the world around him.

January climbed the stairs, but when she got back at the atrium there was no sign of Sklodowska. She left the house in a hurry. After Dr. Jones's speech (or should she say confession?), a visit to the Oneiros Club seemed very urgent indeed.

FOUR

To the uninformed observer, the Oneiros Club is just one more gentleman's club in London, where men gather to drink, smoke, and talk business and other activities usually consigned to masculine territories. Indeed, territories is quite the word, since most of these clubs were founded by explorers or officers of the Empire who had intimate connections with the colonies, such as the East India Club, the Alpine Club, and the Royal Geographic Society. The Oneiros Club is also an explorer's club, even if its members use different maps.

– From *A History of the Oneiros Club*

As a rule, women were not admitted into London gentlemen's clubs. If working as cleaners or scullery maids, they would only gain admittance via the trade entrance. The Oneiros Club, though, was a different matter.

The butler opened the door just enough to show his face, which betrayed some irritation behind the façade of imperturbability:

"The maids' entrance is…"

She didn't deign to speak in response. She just showed her Reassurance.

The Reassurance is the ultimate Oneironaut identity document. It's not quite a card, although it can assume this format. It's a certain symbol customarily drawn on paper, but it can also be etched or engraved in metal or stone. January didn't have time to have it engraved, so she had gone back to her apartment, picked a pen and a blank card, and simply doodled it.

Presumably to save face because of his *faux pas*, the butler took his time squinting, as if to suggest he failed to recognise the symbol for what it was.

Maybe it was for the best. The butler probably didn't have the foggiest idea what an Oneironaut really was. If he had, he would have demanded to be trained as one, thinking (as some do) that he would somehow be able to dream himself away from his wretched existence, emerging in other realities, in a better life. But it didn't work like this, alas.

The impasse, which really wasn't one at all, ended after a couple of minutes, the butler opening the door to allow January passage. She entered a dark hall, with no mirrors and a small marquetry table with a silver tray on it, full of cards and assorted correspondence; she could glimpse a room straight ahead, a bit more illuminated. The butler guided her inside without further comment.

The reading room was rectangular, which meant longer from front to back and a little narrow. There were a few armchairs with lamps, none of them occupied. Huge floor-to-ceiling shelves ran along all the walls, their length broken only by the two doors, the one through which she had just entered, and another, right in front of her at the opposite end of the room, decorated with red baize and closed.

The butler lost no time in going there. She followed swiftly.

As they reached the door, he gestured for her to stop and opened it ever so slightly. Then he entered and announced, in a strangled voice:

"A *female* member, sir."

January could only hear a *harrumph* and see the butler bow. The lights were dim, but she could have sworn he was flushed. The butler then exited and gestured for her to step inside. She entered, to be immediately greeted by a deep, loud voice:

"And who might you be, may I ask?"

The man before her was old and gaunt. He was sitting in a comfortable leather armchair, which looked to be even older than him. He wore a damask robe, and a fez. He was also smoking something sickly-sweet from a long-stemmed pipe. Every time he sucked on the stem, his face became more drawn, maybe due to the big, ugly scar on his right cheek. He was by no means an unpleasant-looking man, but not exactly a handsome one either.

"My name is January Purcell. I am an Oneironaut."

"And why should I take your word for that?"

"I showed the Reassurance at the door."

He shrugged.

"This doesn't *reassure* me of anything. You could have stolen it from a lover."

She cocked her head.

"Do you ask these questions of male travellers?"

"No. Only of members who does not follow proper protocol."

"And this protocol should apply to women but not men?" She smiled. "As I'm sure you know, I am a man as well. Just not here." She thought for a split second if she should finish the remark with a coup de grace, then thought, what the hell? And: "Just as you and all the other Oneironauts who grace the Oneiros Club are also women in other realities. Certainly female Oneironauts cannot be such a rare occurrence here."

The man harrumphed again.

"Regardless of their sex," he said, "the *members* shouldn't be reminded how to behave in the presence of the Director."

Then January put her hand to her bosom and bowed her head in respect.

"I realise now that I was most disrespectful on my entrance. Salaam Aleikum, Mirza Abdullah," she said, adding a curtsy, perhaps a little ironically. The man just bowed his head slightly.

"Aleikum Salaam, Miss Purcell. So you know me, after all."

"Indeed I do, Sir Richard. How could I fail to recognise the great explorer?

Richard Francis Burton – also known as Mirza Abdullah and a host of different names – took his pipe from his mouth, and started glancing around, frowning as if he was missing something. Then, after a couple of minutes, he reached out for a small velvet bag on the side table, and took a pinch of tobacco from inside it. He proceeded, very slowly, to put the tobacco inside the bowl with the help of a slim, long piece of wood, after which he got up and walked right to the fireplace, where he extended the stick until the tip caught fire. Only then did he put it into the bowl, taking the utmost care not to burn the tobacco, but barely brushing the surface of the chamber. Satisfied, he started to suck and puff until January could glimpse a spark above the bowl, and then smoke started to waft out of the pipe and Burton's mouth. The smell was pungent and agreeable to January's nostrils.

"Turkish," she said. "I like it."

Burton puffed appreciatively.

"Quite weak, I know," he said. "As the few Western women I know who enjoy smoking seem to prefer. But, when in Rome… Even though I used to smoke much stronger things."

"Do you miss it?" she asked. "The excitement of the East?"

"I used to, yes. Not now. The dreamworld takes a considerable part of my waking hours. Rome, Miss Purcell, is not only a place, but a reality. This – and he gestured around the smoky room – is our Rome."

"And I need help against the barbarians at the gates," she said.

"What kind of help?"

"I arrived two days ago, and I'm still suffering from quite a bit of lag, I'm afraid. I seem to remember that *Journey to the Centre of the Earth* was purely a book of fiction."

"It is."

"But I have reason to believe Arne Saknussemm was real."

"Not *was*. He *is* real. He is one of us, actually."

"I suspected as much."

"What seems to be the problem? Pray tell."

"I appear to have been attracted here by a certain Dr. Robert Jones, who claims to have built an 'infernal device' of sorts in his dreams. He recruited me and other scientists to go with him to Iceland."

"To go down the Snæfellsjökull, I presume." He coughed. "Damn occlusives. Nordic languages are barbaric." And, suddenly: "Is he one of us, do you think?"

"Untrained, but yes, I see possibilities."

"And what might be the present danger?"

She told him about the experiment in the basement.

"Are you sure that the technology used corresponds to our time period? No borrowings from other timelines?"

"I can't be entirely sure about that," she admitted. "But the fact that he had the whole idea via a dream can't be dismissed. Even if the machinery is entirely ours, the energy released by the diamonds will be unlike anything seen before, and I don't think humankind is able to harness that much power without serious consequences."

Burton frowned. "Were you contacted by another agent? Who gave you this mission?"

She froze. This would be the hardest part of the conversation.

"Nobody. I came here spontaneously."

Burton raised his eyebrows.

"What? How could this happen?"

"I don't know, Sir Richard. Such a thing has never happened to me before."

"I'm not surprised," he said. "Being a novice as you certainly are."

"I have twenty years of experience, Sir Richard."

"Not here."

"I wasn't aware that Oneironauts are to be judged by their time of service in one reality only."

"They are not. I don't believe you, that is all."

"I don't have to prove myself to you. The Higher Power knows the truth of it."

Burton scowled. Seeing the expression of disgust in his face, January knew she wouldn't win this argument. Bringing the Higher Power to the table was a last-ditch effort, and not always an effective one. She shouldn't have resorted to that without a great deal of convincing. Indeed a rookie mistake, as much as she didn't want to acknowledge that.

"Very well," he said, getting up. "Bring me proof, and the resources of the Oneiros Club will be yours."

"I cannot bring you proof until I have returned from Iceland, that is, supposing I can provide proof. You know that."

"I also know that there is no such thing as serendipity in the Long Game, miss!" He spat the words. "I don't know why you have chosen to invade this sanctum sanctorum, but please leave the premises at once." He took a small bronze bell and rang it loudly. The butler opened the door immediately. "I won't say it again."

January left without further comment.

Outside, the wind was blowing a bit too harshly for this time of year. Inside, January was raging. She was well aware of her condition. After all, she didn't just come from another body, no: the process is more complex than this. What happens is a kind of merging of souls – of consciousnesses – so her current incarnation, so to speak, was superseded in part by the memories of being in a man's body in the year 1968. Very vivid memories. In fact, they still endured with such intensity that she sometimes went to the water closet and reached for a penis that was not there. She wasn't sure she envied much of what she had in her previous body, but the ability to urinate while standing was definitely one thing, especially given all these cumbersome clothes.

Also, the nagging feeling that if she were a man here she would have had the ear of Sir Richard Francis Burton, *and* would have been provided with the information she needed so desperately for the mission at hand. Not to mention how she had craved to punch Burton right on that arrogant jaw.

FIVE

"Everybody dreams. Even if you think you don't. You just can't remember. Usually, though, dreams are just dreams. The thing that sets an Oneironaut apart from, say, "normal" people is a matter of access. Oneironauts are able to access a door to a special source of dreams. This source was discovered in the Eighteenth Century by Franz Mesmer, when he was doing research on animal magnetism.

Among other books, he had been reading Plato's Timaeus. This is one of the Greek philosopher's most famous dialogues, in which he makes a distinction between what he calls the physical world and the eternal world. The physical is our world, where everything comes to be, changes, and finally perishes. The eternal world, on the other hand, never changes; it contains everlasting forms or ideals. Take a chair, for instance: an extensive variety of chair can be built in our world – but the original model, the template, if you will, comes from the eternal world. It was always there to start with; we just picked it up from there somehow. Mesmer believed he had discovered where.

This special source received the name of The Existing. Meaning: whatever exists in our world exists first and foremost in this other place."

– From *The Book of Oneiric Rules*

January arrived early at Victoria Station. She took the elevator to the aerodrome. The dirigibles – a whole fleet of them, January counted at least a dozen – were moored to tall, slim pylons. Most people arriving at the station hired porters to carry their baggage. At first, January had thought of carrying only a small knapsack with personal belongings and a bigger bag with clothes and coats. As soon as she got out of the hansom cab, though, she realised that travelling so lightly made her stand out.. She ended up bringing two huge trunks instead. January didn't recall having ever been so prissy in this reality; maybe it was the borrowed time in other bodies.

Mr. Moran waited at the foot of the stairs. He tipped his hat and pointed her the way up the ladder.

The gondola was large – larger than any of the usual dirigibles she had travelled in. January entered via a vestibule, then went down a corridor much larger than in the trains, full of doors to each side.

The first door to the left was open; it led to a spacious meeting room, with an ebony table and eight high-backed chairs. At the far end, Dr. Jones was already there, smoking a cheroot. The window behind him stood open, allowing a brisk breeze to blow into the room.

"Welcome to the *Heathen*, Miss Purcell. Please take a seat."

She sat two chairs away from him.

"Interesting name," she said.

"It is, isn't it? I have a great appreciation of the Arabs and their culture. I've read the Quran and a few texts translated by Burton."

"Do you know Sir Richard?"

"We have met." He pulled some smoke and blew it. "Excited for our trip?"

"Very. When did you two meet?"

He frowned. "At a reception at the British Museum, two years ago. We shared a few memories of the Middle East, but his wife was anxious to leave, so we postponed the rest of the reminiscences for a later day." Then: "Do you know him?"

"We have met," she smiled. "At the Oneiros Club."

Dr. Jones's expression didn't change.

"Never heard of it," he said. "Did they let you in?"

"Not without some difficulty," she admitted. "But I am a full-fledged member."

He smiled. "It must be a very interesting club."

"Quite."

"May I ask what its members must do in order to join? Are they explorers?"

"Of a sort, yes."

"I'm not an explorer, unfortunately," he said. "I've had my fair share of travels around the world, mind. I believe in the power of new experiences, to keep us always on our toes, always fresh, among the real living people. Sometimes, you see, I've felt as if I were living in a dream. The Hindus believe in such a concept, that we are but the dream of Brahma, and when he wakes up this dream will simply dissolve into nothingness." He sighed wistfully. "Even so, I don't feel the inclination to do anything rash, such as Phileas Fogg did. You are aware of his mad adventure, of course?"

"Yes, I am," January answered, thinking, *but I wasn't aware that he was more than a character in a book in this reality.* She suppressed a sigh. "But I do not agree with your self-assessment, Dr. Jones. You are an explorer, after all. Otherwise, why go to Iceland to descend the caldera of an extinct volcano to find diamonds…?"

Jones filled in the rest for her. "…when I could find them abundantly in other places around the world? Why, indeed? I'm not quite sure. I have always had these dreams in which I am doing chivalrous deeds. The interesting thing, though, is that I never dream about castles, fair maidens in distress and shining armour. I once dreamt I was all alone, almost naked, upon a red dust plain, fighting immense spiders, and somehow the fate of Earth depended solely on me." He laughed without any humour; his thin face displayed more a rictus than a real smile, January thought. "Very childish, you see," he said as if excusing himself.

"Not according to Doctor Freud."

"Yes, I've read the Viennese doctor. His thesis on how dreams can be messengers of the unconscious mind is fascinating. I've given it some thought, but in my case I'm afraid the symbolism is very simple, even shallow."

"And what would that symbolism amount to?"

He shrugged. "An unbridled necessity to excel. I'm afraid that's a very common trait for an Etonian."

"That may be true. But dreams rarely are simple. They have unsuspected depths."

"I don't doubt it. As a matter of fact, after my dreams with Saknussemm, I can confirm that you are absolutely right."

"What did these dreams tell you?"

"During the sequence of days in which I had the dream of the tunnel, I saw the alchemist a few times. He showed me with reasonable accuracy the way inside the Diamond Chamber. With Hans' help, I have no doubt we will arrive there soon enough."

"Do you think you will find Saknussemm there?"

"I don't know. But I have the strongest feeling I will find some sort of guidance down there."

January only nodded. Without further help from the Oneiros Club, she would probably have to wait until they reached the volcano to acquire more information. "How many days until we arrive to our destination?"

"Two," Dr. Jones replied. "You will have plenty of time to acclimatise. It's quite cold there."

Indeed, she thought. Plenty of time to get ready for the polar climate – which perhaps wouldn't be so hard, since it was summer. She was well aware this could all be wishful thinking, as she had brought with her only a few pieces of winter apparel.

But she would also have plenty of time to sleep.

SIX

The House is one of the safest manners to enter the Existing. It is not 'a' house, but the ideal house, the essence of a house. That's why each Oneironaut sees it in her own special way, resorting to her memory to create in the mind's eye a very particular point of entry in the Existing.

— From *The Book of Oneiric Rules*

January prepared to enter the dreamstate right after their luncheon over Paris. The weather was cold but fine, with few clouds and a steady wind.

She locked her cabin and started to strip, removing her corset (*bloody thing*, she thought, thanking the Multiplicity of Realities for not requiring her to use this contraption as her other selves) and lying down on her bunk. She closed her eyes and started to breathe slowly.

First, she visualised a white rose, blossoming slowly, unfolding extremely thin, marbled blue-veined petals. The rose swam in her field of vision, shrinking until turning into a cameo. January reached out for it, making the object disappear in her hand.

Then she saw the door.

It was a door like any other, and yet it wasn't. Every time she dives into the dreamstate she faces a different door. The process can be controlled up to a point, but she can't always tell where and when she will end up.

This time, one thing was certain: she wouldn't be back to her Twentieth Century body, not while the male vessel of her consciousness was undergoing surgery. For that reason, she wouldn't be able to project her consciousness upon other realities. But she might be able to open a window, if not a door.

So. She saw a blue window.

January suddenly remembered that this was a window from her childhood (but *which* childhood?). Blue wood with wooden slats: old, smelling of dust and a bit musty. She could see light on the other side, streaming faintly through.

She touched the wood, caressing the slats without hurry – time in the House doesn't run as it does in the Multiplicity of Realities. As always, the feeling was a bit strange, because in that space outside space the Oneironaut doesn't exist in the flesh, but rather in what the Book of Oneiric Rules call the "essence". It was too abstract for her, since she felt pretty much as if she had a body, so she didn't dwell much on this.

Then she opened the window, just enough to peek through. She knew there was a way out, but she wasn't about to go alone.

In this mode, January was a kind of spectator in the landscape of another reality. Almost as if she was in a theatre. So, she watched.

She started to see scenes from another life. But not hers: Dr. Jones'.

At first, she didn't quite understand what she was looking at – until not only her eyes but also her mind, still very much attuned to her male counterpart, adjusted. And she understood: she was indeed in a theatre, but one that was bigger, much better illuminated than those she was accustomed to. There was music playing, loud music. Incredibly loud music, and somewhat dissonant. Yet, she found it appealing, maybe because her male version used to listen to this kind of music. It was called rock and roll.

The stage was filled with musicians and instruments, all of which were illuminated from above, with lights of many colours: green, blue, red, yellow, some of them waving like palm fronds, some pulsing in rhythm with the music.

Then, someone else entered the stage. A tall, very white man dressed in extravagant clothes, even for the future. Was it a man, though? The figure was so wavy and sinewy, and he also walked on high heels, swaying his hips wildly.

But the face. The face was unmistakable. She would recognise it everywhere. Everywhen.

Dr. Jones.

Only it wasn't him. It was another version of him, projected into a future age in similar fashion to her male version, who was even now on the operating table.

Suddenly, she had the strangest feeling. It was as if she was being observed behind her back. She spun around quickly.

Nothing.

But the corridor was somehow a tad darker – as if there was something or someone beyond, blocking the light.

It wasn't usual for two people to be in the House simultaneously – for there was a House for every Oneironaut. This *could* happen, though, when an apprentice travelled in dreams along with her instructor.

Or when someone invaded the Existing.

When she (or her male counterpart) started practicing to become an agent, January heard of a few cases where older students played pranks on the novices. In fact, she only heard of one case – because it had ended tragically.

Her heart started beating faster.

January didn't want to stay to see who might be there: she exited the House via the back door, just in case. And woke up.

She stayed in her bed, immobile but restless, pondering what to do next.

SEVEN

One thing you must always keep in mind when entering the Existing is: time passes differently there. There is no such thing as linear time. One can spend your whole life thinking otherwise, so long as you never experience the dreamstate. The Oneironaut must take care when travelling between realities and always return by the same reality she came from. This is called retreading. Also: during a mission, avoid sleeping when not retreading, so you don't get entwined in different realities. You may want to use the Rest Room in the House for your safety.

– From *The Book of Oneiric Rules, Revised Edition*

Time seemed to pass quickly once they arrived in Iceland. On their way to the volcano, January could barely remember the briefing Dr. Jones gave them just before the dirigible docked at Reykjavik Central Station. Later, it would come to her in flashes.

"Very well," he said when all of them had joined him at the meeting room. "Here's a schedule, to be followed once we dock, along with a brief description of every member's responsibilities."

"First: we will meet Hans at the station, from where we will proceed to the volcano by train and coach."

"I beg your pardon," January interrupted, "but wouldn't it be easier to just meet the guide here and continue travelling by dirigible?"

At that, Dr. Jones bared his teeth slightly; an expression that January though initially might be a smile, but then realised was a grimace of disgust, as if he was smelling something rotten. Before he had the chance to speak, however, Mr. Moran hastened to explain.

"I'm afraid that's not possible, Miss Purcell", he said. "The weather in the region of the volcano is very unstable, with plenty of drafts and more than the occasional storm, so it's swifter and safer to travel by land. I'm sure you can understand that," he finished, with more than a hint of condescendence.

January wished she could punch both their smiles out of existence, but she simply nodded in agreement.

"We should arrive there in approximately eight hours after touching ground," Dr. Jones said. "Then we will divide into two groups. I will go down Skartaris with Mr. Moran, while Misses Sklodowska and Purcell will stay at the entrance monitoring the levels of energy with the device."

January flinched violently. But Sklodowska's reaction was harsher: she stood up and shouted: "*Non!*"

"I beg your pardon?" Jones said.

"Frankly, *mon cher* Jones, I didn't come all the way from Paris to London, *and* from London to Iceland, to be dismissed. You hired me to work for you as a physicist, and as such I am perfectly capable of doing my job wherever I am required, as long as I have the necessary equipment. You, I see, have shipped part of this equipment with us on this journey; *Donc*, I must insist in going down with you, because I really don't know what good is going to be in staying on the surface taking *des mesures*. What sort of measurements can a chemist do far from her object of study? *Très absurde*, I say. Also, I can hike and climb mountains as well as any man. And it's *Docteur* Sklodowska, not Miss."

Dr. Jones listened to her with mouth slightly agape. His bad eye squinted a bit, and January could swear she saw something of a gleam on it, as if it had caught a stray beam of sunlight. But the sun had just set and the lamps in the room hadn't been lit yet.

"To that, Dr. Jones," she quickly added, with the tiniest smile, "I can only add that you will need a geologist to assess the purity of any diamonds you find down there. After all, it is hard for an untrained mind to tell the difference between a diamond in the rough and a mere quartz crystal, let alone in the near darkness of a cave system."

"Very well," Dr. Jones finally said after a few seconds. "If you insist, you shall go with us. I have neither the time nor the disposition to argue. But I must warn you: I won't listen to any complaints regarding the roughness of the journey."

"There will be none," Sklodowska said. January shook her head in solidarity with the Polish scientist's words.

"Very well then," Dr. Jones said, getting up. January could swear he was a bit shaky. "We will have plenty of time to talk about it when we get there. I'm going to my private quarters for some rest. You will be called when we start the docking procedures." And with that he left. January looked after him, but all she could see was a glimpse of Mr. Moran's eyes as he followed Dr. Jones.

Dr Jones was distraught. *There is something eating him*, January thought, and she could guess what it was.

"Don't you think there is something strange about him?" Sklodowska asked her suddenly.

"Why, yes," January answered. "Did you notice too?"

"He is becoming increasingly agitated. Did you notice how his pupils were dilated? I think he didn't have much sleep these past few days."

January nodded. "You're right."

"Another thing," Sklodowska added. "Did you notice that both Dr. Jones and Mr. Moran occupy the same sleeping quarters?"

"No," January answered, a bit upset, already knowing where the conversation was going. "But is this relevant?"

"Yes, but this ship is the property of Dr. Jones; he probably has his own quarters, even in this airship."

January lifted a brow.

"What they do behind closed doors is none of our concern, Miss Sklodowska."

Sklodowska grimaced.

"I'm not implying anything unbecoming, Miss Purcell," she said. "Nor was I thinking of such things. Even though love between men is considered sinful in Poland, it is somewhat trivial in the Parisian *bas-fond*. This is not what concerns me. What I was trying to say is of quite a different nature."

"And what is that?"

"I have reason to believe Mr. Moran might be poisoning Dr. Jones."

January only nodded. For a fraction of a second, she thought Sklodowska was a fellow Oneironaut. But she didn't have the *physique du rôle* to be one. She didn't sport the marks of one well-travelled through the dreamways. As it was, she couldn't confide in her. But Sklodowska was not only an extremely intelligent woman, she also seemed street savvy, her comments not to be dismissed lightly.

"Why do you think that?" she asked, though she already knew very well what her colleague was talking about.

"His complexion is different. It's been changing very softly, since the day I first met him. That happened two days before you came. Despite his thinness, he had colour in his cheeks and a spring in this step, so to speak... He was very excited by his discovery, and he could barely refrain from dancing."

"Dancing?"

Sklodowska smiled.

"Yes. I know he looks like a serious man, but I can assure you that's not the case at all. I had known him briefly when he visited me in Paris. I was working with Pierre until the end of our engagement..."

"Oh, I am terribly sorry," January blurted.

"About what?"

"The end of your engagement."

Sklodowska laughed.

"Oh, that? Don't be sorry, *mon amie*. Our research was more important than any romantic considerations. When Dr. Jones approached me, I couldn't refuse his offer. Pierre and I remain friends, though."

January could only nod. For she – or rather, her male counterpart – remembered very well that Marie Sklodowska married Pierre Curie and became famous all over the world using her husband's surname.

"When Dr. Jones appeared," Sklodowska continued, "he wanted to know more about the work we were doing in our lab regarding new substances. After the Cavor Scandal, he, as many other capitalists, started to believe that new substances were easy to create."

January blinked. Her other self's presence was still very strong here. She couldn't, for the life of her, remember whether the whole story H. G. Wells described on *The First Men in the Moon* was true. As far as she recalled, in the world where her male counterpart lived –

and where he was being operated on now – all those characters were entirely fictional.

She hated asking questions, even – especially – if she were lost. But it could be significant.

"I'm sorry. I'm familiar with Dr. Cavor, but I've been out of the country and I can't seem to remember having read any news about this scandal."

"He is no doctor, I can assure you of that. At least I know *I* am deserving of the title." January remained quiet at that diatribe. "*Mister* Cavor approached a capitalist and offered him a new substance, cavorite, which he guaranteed would enable anyone to travel to the moon and the stars." She made a face. "A few months after the capitalist's announcement, he said to a newspaper that everything had been just an elaborate hoax, but Mr. Cavor had recognised the error of his ways and retired to the country, so he wouldn't pursue charges. Word has it that what really happened is that Cavor took his own life. Well, good riddance to him."

January tsked internally. If this reality strictly followed the plots of the novels she had read, then Cavor would be with the selenites as they spoke, or he had most probably died of the flu and taken the entire population of the moon with him. A veritable shame.

But there was nothing she could do about this. Not now, at any rate.

"But can you create a substance?" she asked instead.

"Not exactly. You can create compounds, mixing elements. Like steel, which is an alloy of iron and carbon. Bronze, pewter, brass – they are all alloys. They were created in the search for durability, strength, or resistance to corrosion and other things related to industry and construction. But an entirely new element, and with antigravitational powers? That nobody saw it was a scam all along leaves me infuriated, to be honest."

"And you were able to explain it to Dr. Jones? I mean, did he listen to you?"

"Yes. After a bit of trouble and some reassurance by Pierre, naturally. Men," she huffed. "He wanted to manufacture a substitute for coal, which in itself is a commendable thing. In fact, he wanted to create a new species of diamond."

"A new mineral?"

"Or a kind of alloy that possesses the same characteristics," she said. "That is, some kind of material that could be 'milked'" and she mimicked the hand gestures of a farmer who milks a cow, "of its intrinsic energy."

"It seems strangely reminiscent of alchemy to me, don't you think?"

Sklodowska smiled.

"I agree," she said. "But chemistry is alchemy by other means. 'Rien ne se perd, rien ne se crée, tout se transforme'."

"'Nothing is lost, nothing is created, everything is transformed.' Lavoisier."

"By way of Anaxagoras."

"Do we know how he died? Because Lavoisier lost his head."

Sklodowska laughed out loud.

"Anaxagoras died in exile, as far as we know. In a way, we're already exiles, so let's take care not to lose our heads following Dr. Jones."

EIGHT

"In order to enter the Existing, Oneironauts must perform autogenic training, a relaxation technique that facilitates concentration and focus. There are three basic steps in this training:

1. Sensory deprivation

2. Mental repetition of verbal formulae

3. Passive concentration

The first step can be done via Vipassana meditation, in which the Oneironaut closes his eyes and blanks his mind. The second is easily reached by the repetition of a mantra, which can be a sentence or even a word, regardless if the Oneironaut knows the meaning of what's being said (what matters is the intention). The third is also acquired via meditation, more particularly the technique of labelling sensations and thoughts that come and go through the mind of the meditator."

– From The Book of Oneiric Rules

The rest of the trip went quickly. They met Hans in the station and immediately took the train to the region of the volcano. The guide was amiable and kept them entertained during most of the five-hour journey, talking mostly about Verne's book.

"Verne didn't interview me, as I later learned he had Professor Lidenbrock," he said, and laughed. "But I don't mind. It made me famous."

He was a big, burly man. But not in the pedestrian way Verne described him, which had made him seem silly, even mentally challenged. Granted, Hans was older now, and he sported a salt-and-pepper beard that made him look wiser than his years. Gertrude was nowhere to be seen. Sklodowska asked him about the duck.

Another laugh. "It was a complete fabrication! I never had a pet duck named Gertrude. What I had was a pet goose named Rex, but that was when I was a very young boy. When I started working with my father, I didn't have time for pets and other childhood things."

"What can you tell us about the Centre of the Earth?" January asked.

"Why, nothing."

"Nothing?"

"We never reached the Centre of the Earth. It was very hot down there. But we went down all right – many miles."

"And what did you find there?"

"Not much. A few animals, very strange ones. Most of them didn't have eyes. But this happened deeper down."

"The thing we're after," interrupted Dr. Jones, "is on an earlier level."

"Yes," Hans concurred. "Much more illuminated."

At that observation, Dr. Jones tapped his nose, and Hans nodded knowingly.

"We will arrive there at night," Hans said. "We are going to sleep and then set out early in the morning, after a good rest and breakfast."

"I'm afraid that will not be possible," Dr. Jones said, seeming a bit uncomfortable. January noted the tiniest drop of sweat running down his right temple. "We must proceed immediately with the plan."

Hans became very serious.

"Dr. Jones, I know how eager you are to get down there, but let me assure you this is not an easy task. Monsieur Verne made it sound far easier than it really was. We will have to achieve the top of Skartaris and then skirt around at least a third of its diameter before we reach the top of the volcano. This alone will take us more than a few hours, and we will be very tired. We must rest at the entrance of the tunnel before descending. There's a plateau there, sloping a little, but with a smooth, level stretch that is very good for resting."

"We will see about that when we get there," Dr. Jones said, and pulled out his watch. "There remain a couple of hours before we arrive. I suggest we all get a little rest, so that we can rise up to the challenge reinvigorated."

They all went to their respective cabins. January shared with Sklodowska, so she didn't have the privacy required to meditate and properly reach the dreamstate. Anyway, she didn't feel she would need more than a good rest before the rough part of the trip began in earnest. She closed her eyes.

And opened them suddenly to see Mr. Moran leaning over her. In her cabin!

She jumped to her feet, showing quick reflexes – reflexes she didn't know she had in that reality. Mr. Moran seemed more startled than her.

"By God, Miss Purcell," he said, shuffling hastily backwards.

"What are you doing here?" she asked, still maintaining the fighting stance. Moran held his hands up.

"I was sent by Dr. Jones to tell you we shall be arriving at Helissandur in a short while. You might want to freshen up and join us at the restaurant car."

Realising she remained ready to attack, January relaxed her stance, though she remained wary of this man who had entered her cabin without permission.

"Very well, though you might consider knocking next time." She drew a deep breath and said, "Thank you. We will be there shortly."

Mr. Moran departed without another word. January sat back in her cot, only to see that Sklodowska had been watching her all along.

"Where did you learn that?" she asked her.

"My brother." It was all January could think of. In a way, her male counterpart could easily be considered a brother-in-arms.

"Do it again," Sklodowska said.

"I beg your pardon?"

"Do it one more time, please."

January got up and repeated the stance. Sklodowska got up too – and touched January's extended right arm. "You should relax your shoulder," she said, taking the elbow and pulling it ever so slightly towards January's chest, folding the arm a little. "This should help you to withstand any impact. But I must say your feet are very well grounded. Well done."

"How do you know all that?" January asked.

Sklodowska shrugged, smiling. "I have a brother too." And, going to the door: "We should hurry. Maybe there's time for a cup of coffee and a tart? I'm famished."

January followed her, speechless, feeling as if she hadn't quite woken up. Everything around her seemed a bit hazy, and the strange situation back in their cabin had done nothing to make her feel better.

They arrived at the restaurant car and promptly sat across from Dr. Jones, Mr. Moran and Hans. January looked through the window; there was a bit of frost smudging the glass. She stopped for a moment, breathing slowly, and allowed herself to smile upon seeing the blanket of snow covering the land. She couldn't see Snæfellsjökull from here, but as soon as the train stopped they would get a coach straight there, and then start in earnest their own journey-to-not-quite-the-centre-of-the-Earth.

"Are you tired?" she heard a voice behind her ask.

When she turned, everything was dark. She was exhausted after seven hours in the coach and trekking the rough trail leading to the volcanic tube of Snæfellsjökull. It was as if she hadn't got any sleep at all.

The entire trip so far had been made under cover of night, and they were using Coleman torches to illuminate the way ahead. January was still feeling dizzy, and a bit hungry at that. The others didn't look any different; they made the whole surface trip in a moody silence. Dr. Jones looked the worst of them; he seemed even thinner and paler than during the trip, if such a thing were possible. His hands shook a little.

Maybe it was the effort of climbing, she thought. But he seemed to her eyes incredibly similar to someone who was suffering mild withdrawal symptoms.

So, not poisoning as Sklodowska had surmised. Addiction, more likely. The question remained, though: was the drug administered by Jones himself? Or could it be that Moran was giving it to him? And, if so, why?

Dr. Jones was too quiet. Moran was hovering very near, looking at him, more as a watchdog than a caretaker. January approached him cautiously.

"Are you all right?" she asked, putting her fingertips on his wrist.

By the light of the torch, he was incredibly pale indeed. He looked sick. Eyes hooded as if he was under the influence of opium. She had never seen him like this before, not this wasted. She couldn't believe it was the poppy. It leaves traces, vestiges she would recognise. They weren't there.

"I will be fine soon," Dr. Jones answered.

"Now," said Hans, starting to build a fire. "We rest. Otherwise we won't be able to make this journey properly."

Dr. Jones only nodded, finally agreeing with the guide. He was clearly exhausted.

January looked intently at him. She wanted to talk to him without anyone close, so she could be open, at least in part, and to explain everything she could about the Oneironauts, and of the impending doom she sensed. She wasn't feeling good about this trip – even if, as far as she could feel, the journey wasn't going to be exactly harmful to them as a group. It could very well, though, trigger a series of events that would be damaging to others, on a larger scale.

Not quite the end of the world, not literally. But kind of.

But then Moran approached him.

"Excuse me, Dr. Jones. Time for your medication."

Jones looked up and smiled weakly at January.

"Let's rest then, shall we? We'll need our strength to make this journey."

She obliged, getting up and going back to Sklodowska. Together, they unpacked sleeping bags and got inside them. They made their camp right inside the lip of the tunnel, so they would be shielded from the wind. Now the fire was high, and they could sleep, if fitfully.

January pondered. Would she be able to visit Burton in a lucid dream? This would be a tricky undertaking. She was also feeling a bit weakened by the continuous travelling. She consulted her watch. Two a.m. By her calculations, it would also be the early hours in London, which meant Burton was likely to be asleep.

NINE

One of the most dangerous situations for an Oneironaut is what we call the Butterfly Dream. This is a parable written by the Taoist philosopher Chuang-tzu three centuries before Jesus Christ and two centuries after the Buddha, that goes like this: "Once upon a time, I, Chuang-tzu, dreamt I was a butterfly, fluttering hither and thither, to all intents and purposes a butterfly. I was conscious only of my happiness as a butterfly, unaware that I was Chuang-tzu. Soon I awakened, and there I was, veritably myself again. Now I do not know whether I was then a man dreaming I was a butterfly, or whether I am now a butterfly, dreaming I am a man." It still remains to be seen if Chuang-tzu was an Oneironaut, but he described very well what it means to be trapped in dreams within dreams, where the dream traveller must be wary else she will find herself unable to distinguish between illusion and reality.

— From In Libro Somnium

Afghanistan in May is incredibly hot. Temperatures can easily reach 50 degrees Celsius during the day. Even in shade, the heat is enough for a non-native to suffer a heatstroke. Even in Band-e Amir.

The region, famous for its beautiful lakes and oases, is one of the most beautiful in the whole world. This is the opinion of Sir Richard Francis Burton, in whose dream January happens to be dwelling.

As such, January doesn't feel the heat. This is really a dream, not another reality.

But, by sheer force of will, she can make it as vivid as if she were in fact living there. Maybe the things are more real to her than to Burton himself, who's dressed like a native. In fact, he looks so much like one that January only recognises him because it's his dream, and he stands out from the rest of the landscape like a sore thumb.

"I come here frequently," he says without turning back. January is only mildly impressed.

"I didn't know you could will yourself a particular dreamscape," she says. Which is a bald lie. She never did this, but she knows it's been done many times before. Naturally, Burton knows she knows.

"You probably know I loathe to be interrupted in my leisure. What do you want?"

"Information."

"Regarding what?"

"Did you already know that Robert Jones is a potential Oneironaut?"

"Every human – and many a non-human – is a potential Oneironaut."

"It would have helped me to know more about him beforehand."

"I suppose you can consult the Tomes tomorrow, if you want."
She sighs.

"That will be quite hard to do. I'm in Iceland."

"When you come back, then."

"Can you help me with one more thing?"

"If I may be of assistance."

"His personal valet, Mr. Moran – there is something about him I don't like."

"And?"

"Is he aware of all this?" she gestured to the dream.

"I don't know. Never met him. Maybe you can find something about him in the Tomes."

"Can I visit the Club now?"

"In your dreams? No."

"Maybe if you could go with me…"

"I don't need to remind you that you are intruding. You invaded my personal dream. There is nothing for you here. As I said, when you come back to London you may go the Club again. Now that I know you are one of us, you will have free access to the Tomes. Goodbye."

She woke up. Already in motion. She shook her head in disbelief. How was it possible? January had the sensation of not having got any sleep at all since she disembarked from Dr. Jones' airship. But, if her head was still woozy, at least the descent was smooth.

The ground ahead sloped downward just a bit, making the journey easy for the group. Hans led the way, followed a dozen yards behind by Dr. Jones, who seemed much better after the night's rest, but even so Mr. Moran was constantly at his side, never touching him, but talking close to his ear, as if encouraging him to go on. January followed close behind, with Sklodowska, who seemed particularly excited.

"This is marvellous," she said. "The temperature here is warm, but only slightly. I almost feel like taking my coat off." She was wearing a fur coat. Too thick for January's tastes. She favoured lighter, coarser materials, preferring to wear a leather coat.

"If the gradient remains as gentle as this, it will take us quite some time before we feel real heat," she said. "In fact, if there is a real cave system down there, it's probably very drafty, so I would say that the chance of us feeling hot is small."

"I can only hope we don't take too long to get there," Sklodowska said.

"I wouldn't worry too much about that."

"Why do you say such things, *ma chère amie*? We've been descending this path for two days now."

This was just wrong, January thought. Suddenly she couldn't stand it any more. She stopped and grabbed Sklodowska by the arm.

"Are you joking?" she asked the Polish scientist. "If so, I can assure you this is *not* funny."

"What do you mean?"

"Are you giving me the same drug you gave to Dr. Jones?"

"What are you talking about?"

"You know very well what I'm talking about."

"Ladies, please!" Hans' cheery voice was now tinged with a concerned tone. "Do not stray away from us. Let's all keep together."

By the light of the Coleman lantern she carried, Sklodowska seemed worried as well.

"He is right, you know. I don't want to get lost in these tunnels."

"What tunnels?"

Sklodowska muttered something unintelligible under her breath. Probably a curse in Polish, January thought.

"You mean you don't remember?"

"I don't remember having started the descent. In fact, I can't recall lots of things, including sleeping." *And I could desperately use some sleep,* she thought too, but didn't say out loud.

"We should be going," Sklodowska said. "But don't worry. According to what Hans told us this morning, we should reach our destination in a few hours. Then you can explain to me what you are feeling, and you will also be able to have some rest."

January started walking, right behind Sklodowska. She wasn't sure of anything now. The light of the lantern threw long, distorting shadows over the walls of the cave, but she couldn't really tell if she was dreaming or awake.

Maybe she was stuck inside someone else's dream? But she was able to sleep just before entering the volcanic tube, and get herself inside Burton's dream. On the other hand, she didn't appear to be having any sleep, and to dream she would have to sleep. Was someone in the expedition deliberately hampering her efforts?

Sklodowska seemed innocent enough. She dismissed Hans because they had just met, and nothing in his behaviour betrayed any knowledge of such things. Mr. Moran was a possible candidate, but he kept mostly to himself, so she didn't have enough data. The only person she could think of was Dr. Jones himself, but he still didn't know how to access his abilities. She would have to confront him as soon as they reached their destination.

This took a few hours, as Sklodowska had promised. Their watches measured the time, since they obviously couldn't see if it was day or night out there. They walked slowly but surely, stopping only to answer the call of nature, which was something of a hurdle in the wilderness (and the interior of a cave system is as much a wilderness as the African veldt or the Amazon jungle); since Hans didn't want anyone to stray from the group – apparently this had happened during his first journey, or so he implied – they had to stop every three or four hours and organise, taking the utmost care not to turn off the lamps nor to illuminate too much what shouldn't be brought to light.

So they arrived, in the morning of the third day down there (that's what Sklodowska had said, but for January only a few hours had passed since they the airship docked in Reykjavik), at the first crossroads.

During the first day of the journey (as Sklodowska explained to January, who had no recollection of that time), Hans had filled them with more details of the Lidenbrock expedition. Among the things they found down there were several markers left by Arne Saknussemm. The old alchemist had carved sigils in the stone of the walls: circles with arrows pointing in the direction which he had taken, and the letters AS below them. In the first crossroads, the sigil was on the left pathway. So, they took it.

This would be repeated half a dozen times during the third day. January tried to memorise the way into the labyrinth, but gave up after the fourth sigil. She was starting to feel the heat. The interesting thing, though, was that her fingers touched the stone of the walls and felt only cold. Was she sick?

"This is strange," Hans said, taking off his coat. "I don't recall it being so hot here this early."

Sklodowska tut-tutted.

"Are you familiar with the concept of radiation?" she whispered to January.

"Yes," she answered, though she couldn't quite tell Sklodowska that she had read a lot about her counterpart Marie Curie, and her death by exposure to radioactive materials in another reality.

"This heat is of a similar nature. Not radiation from the sun, but from some kind of mineral."

"Do you think we are approaching a deposit of quap?"

"I don't know. Though it seems the only possible explanation at this point."

Then Dr. Jones collapsed.

Mr. Moran was alert enough not to let him fall to the ground. He wrapped a hand around Dr. Jones's midsection and practically carried him for half a dozen metres, until they got to a sort of ledge, where they sat.

"We should spend the night here," Hans said.

"No," Dr. Jones replied. "It's just the heat. I will rest for a while and then we will be on our way again."

"I must insist, Dr. Jones."

"I will carry him if necessary," Mr. Moran said.

"There will be no need for this," a voice boomed from the other side of the ledge. A voice that didn't belong to any of them.

January shivered as if the voice was made of ice needles prickling her scalp. Sklodowska just stayed where she was, as if frozen. Hans turned abruptly the torch in the direction of the strange voice.

It was an angel.

That, at least, was January's first impression, which she immediately attributed to her Church of England upbringing. Because of course it wasn't an angel, it couldn't be: such things didn't exist, she knew that. But this was unlike anything she had ever seen in her life: very tall (she guessed seven and a half feet tall, maybe eight), skin very pale, almost like alabaster, and hair the same: long, falling over his shoulders. She was pretty certain the figure was male.

He wore a kind of toga, draped over naked shoulders. Initially she thought he was barefoot, but then saw that in fact he wore thin, colourless sandals.

"I see you are exhausted," the figure went on. "We can provide rest and food for you."

"'We'?" asked January. "'We' who?"

The figure curved his lips upward. In an ordinary human, this would have passed for a smile. In this instance January found the expression incredibly unsettling.

"We are the Vril-Ya. And this," he gestured encompassing the tunnels, "is where my race lives."

Then Dr. Jones got up and took off his hat.

"Magistrate An, I presume," he said. "I am Doctor Robert Jones, and I seek your assistance."

January had not seen that coming.

TEN

The Long Game is as intricate as the Great Game — with a devious twist regarding the notion of reality: one of the most vicious stratagems within it is the Feint, where one agent tries to convince his adversary that he is not wrong for political reasons, but for the simple fact that he is not an Oneironaut, because there is no such thing as dream-travelling, and that he in fact is a patient in a sanitarium. Bedlam, as we know, is full of our enemies.

— From Sir Richard Francis Burton's private journals

Magistrate An (now January knew for sure the exquisite creature was a he) led them down a small ramp to a kind of valley, which was just beyond the promontory. January would have missed the ramp entirely if the Vril-ya (was there a singular, or did the name of the race remains unchanged? She didn't want to ask) hadn't suddenly turned left behind a boulder.

They followed him for almost thirty minutes. Distances could be deceiving underground. Until they arrived at the Pale City.

The real name of the place was unpronounceable. The city was a big, sprawling agglomeration of low buildings, not dissimilar to the habitations of American Pueblo Indians. But the Magistrate's clothes looked more Roman or Greek.

One thing they immediately noticed was the utter lack of colour. Every single thing in the city was white or grey. January could see everything in stark detail, though she couldn't for the life of her work out where the light came from.

"Remarkable," Sklodowska said under her breath. "They seem to emit light themselves, as some creatures of the deep sea do. I wonder if they are radioactive."

"Are we in any danger, do you think?" January asked.

"Not likely. If they are healthy, as seems to be the case, then they suffered enough mutation along the generations to render their luminosity a hereditary trait but not damaging. On the other hand,"

and she cocked her head thoughtfully, "there's a lot of endogamy around, as far as I can see. Their bodies are huge, and they have all the same fenotype."

"Certainly no black people here."

"Nor red. Nor yellow."

"Or white, for that matter," boomed the Magistrate's voice again. "We resemble you, but we are not human in any conceivable way, my friends. We are another race entirely. A separate evolution, if you will."

"Have you lived here always?" Sklodowska asked him.

"No," the Magistrate answered while walking ahead of them. "We lived on the surface millennia ago, until a series of cataclysms made us search for the safety that can only be truly found under the Earth. There is no end to the wonders here."

"We are here precisely because of that," Dr. Jones said.

"I know. We have been waiting for you. The Alchemist visited us."

Then Jones smiled.

"He told me of you as well."

January frowned.

"Wait," she said. "Are you talking about Arne Saknussemm?"

"That is his name, yes."

"But he is dead," she said. "I mean, he was born two hundred years ago."

"That is true," said the Magistrate. "However, he contacted us via the Stream, where time is not an obstacle."

"What is this?" she asked.

"In due time, I will show you. Now you are my guests, and will have my hospitality." He gestured for them to enter one of the buildings.

To January, those words sounded more like a menace than an invitation.

"What is this all about?" Dr. Jones suddenly appeared by her side. "What are you saying about Saknussemm?"

"What I know about him," she said.

"And what do you know?"

January only hesitated briefly, but the Magistrate interrupted before she could give any kind of reply.

"You are going to stay in this guesthouse," he said, this time in a tone that left January in no doubt of his intentions. "As you can see, there is plenty of food and drink for you, and beds if you want to rest. I must attend to urgent matters, but I will return in a few hours." And he left. The door was locked behind him.

"We are prisoners," January said.

"Not for long," Dr. Jones said, though without much conviction. "What did you mean, then?"

"I could ask you the same thing, Dr. Jones. What is happening?"

"I am here on a mission, Miss Purcell. So far, the mission is proceeding according to plan. Now, could you tell me what your part is supposed to be in all this? Because, let me be frank: you are not here to help further the advancement of science, are you? Are you an agent of the Crown?"

"I am indeed an agent, Dr. Jones, but not of the Crown. In effect I am an agent of the Empire, though it would be more accurate to say it in the plural."

"Empires? Are you a double agent, then?"

"Do you work for the Russians?" Mr. Moran asked. "Or the Ottomans?"

"No," she said. "I work for a higher power."

"And this higher power is intent on stopping me?"

If January were to be honest, she would have to admit she just didn't know. But she couldn't afford honesty, not when they were in the hands of a potential enemy.

"We don't stop anyone," she said. "We merely observe."

He smiled ironically. "You are, then, in the most privileged seat of the audience."

Suddenly Sklodowska laughed.

"Will you be capable of merely observing while imprisoned?" she asked ruefully. January was intrigued.

"What do you mean?"

Sklodowska looked at her with condescendence.

"You can drop it, my dear. I already told him you are an Oneironaut."

"What?" January said. "How do you know that?" The time for pretence was clearly past.

"Ah, you see," Sklodowska said, "I am one who knows."

Dr. Jones smiled at that.

"You clearly know your John Donne, my dear," he said. "It's quite delightful."

January felt like slapping both of them.

"But why?"

"I could ask you the same question," Sklodowska said. "Why did you become a member of the Fellowship?"

January shrugged. It was a good question, but she didn't have time to answer it fully now.

"Why didn't you?" she chose to retort.

"Because there were other options," Sklodowska said as if it was only natural. "The Existing isn't property of the Fellowship. Every human being should be able to learn how to access it. That's what I've been doing. And I'm not alone."

"Saknussemm was working with you, then."

"*Exactement.*"

"So you and your fellow anarchists have been wreaking havoc all this time."

"For the record, we prefer to call ourselves Anarchronists," she said with a tight-lipped smile.

January frowned.

"A bit too flamboyant, perhaps?" Sklodowska asked her.

"I was thinking of *childish*, instead."

Sklodowska shrugged.

"It doesn't matter what you think. The word is fitting enough. So are our intentions. Which are peaceful, by the way."

"Manipulating people and events?"

"No." Sklodowska's expression was serious now. "Steering people. Helping them fulfill their potential. As I have been doing with David ever since he came to me in Paris."

"David?"

Sklodowska smiled.

"His full name is David Robert Jones. His current self prefers to be called Robert. But I call him David because that's what he prefers to be called in all the other realities."

"So you know all that," January turned to Dr. Jones.

"I do," he said. "But I can't remember anything. Marie told me I would need to be trained if I wanted to recall my dreams."

"Your realities," Sklodowska corrected him.

Dr. Jones nodded.

"I just wish," he said, "I could have dreamt myself in here without having to travel, as I did before. Why wasn't that possible?"

"I already told you that you were really dreaming then," Sklodowska said, but he was looking at January.

She answered, "There are many kinds of dreams... David." Normal people usually have normal dreams, full of imagery from the unconscious. Once in a while, though, you can have a different sort of lucid dream, where things are more concrete and coherent. But only a trained Oneironaut can access the Existing and from there a beachhead to different realities. Now, for instance, we are in a lucid dream." And, turning to Sklodowska: "Is it yours or his?"

"What do you mean?" Dr. Jones asked. "We're not dreaming."

"We are," January said. "I recognize the signs. The fuzzy edges in the borders of my vision, a certain light-headedness, and something many of my counterparts call "jumpcuts". It's a movie-related thing, which you haven't seen yet, but the gist is that you sometimes move from one place to the next without quite knowing how it happened. Didn't you notice that?"

Dr. Jones frowned. "I seem to remember our journey well. The air trip was remarkably fine for this time of year. The train was too slow, I'm afraid."

"But the climbing," Sklodowska said slowly, as if noticing something suddenly. "I can't remember much of it."

As I tried to tell you back there, January thought. "It wasn't you, then?"

"No."

"Could it be you, Dr. Jones? Did you dream all of this? The same way you dreamt your meetings with that remarkable man?"

He shook his head adamantly.

"Not at all," he said. "How could I?"

You can more than many of us, she thought. But she didn't have time to reply. Mr. Moran coughed politely.

"Allow me to explain," he said, pointing a gun at them. "This dream is mine."

Interlude

In the streets of London, Davey Jones runs.

He was on his way to the studio to record a few songs. He shouldn't be late — he paid for it, with a few friends. They want to be famous. It's something he has been craving for all his life. He's twenty-one in Swinging London, and he thinks he's too old to make it big.

But now a dear friend is fighting for his life.

He doesn't have many friends. Somehow, he knows he will always be a lonely man. So, he cherishes the few good friends he has.

He received the news a couple of hours ago. His friend was shot and is going through major surgery in the City. Davey is just a poor boy and had to take a train from Bromley, but he's arrived at Victoria Station and is now running the few hundred metres between the station and the hospital.

He met JP at a party. They got along very easily. JP was a little older than Davey, an interesting man, a mix of suave and rugged, something between Sean Connery and Alain Delon, if such a mixture were possible. All Davey knew was that he was pretty much shaken AND stirred by this man. He was beginning to experiment with drugs and sex. Even though he hadn't been in bed with JP, he wouldn't mind doing so.

But things didn't go exactly that way. He found out that JP was some sort of agent, and, even though that excited him, it also scared him shitless. He wasn't really sure if he wanted to mingle with someone involved in death and mayhem, so to speak.

Sometimes, though, you end up involved all the same.

His first lucid dream with this man was something from another world. They had met in a fantastical city which made Davey think of Fritz Leiber's books. He had read a couple of Fafhrd and the Gray Mouser stories, and for him the ancient city, with its golden spires and cobbled streets, was reminiscent of Lankhmar.

"Not quite," JP said. Davey looked down and saw that both of them were dressed in khakis, with pith helmets to boot.

"At least we're not dressed like heathens," Davey blurted, without knowing why he had just said that.

"This is quite interesting," JP told him, frowning. "You were not supposed to be here. Are you a spontaneous, I wonder?"

"Spontaneous? I'm not sure I know what you mean."

"Have you experienced this kind of dream before?" he asked.

David pondered.

"A few times during my adolescence, yes. I usually dreamed of the Middle and Far East, usually in Victorian times. I was quite a dapper gentleman, by the way... and once I recall having dreamed about another planet. I seem to recall having dreamt with you once too, but you were a woman," he said tongue-in-cheek.

JP didn't laugh.

"I don't recall that," he said, "but it may lie in my future. I might have to introduce you to a friend of mine, but not now. Please wake up."

Davey woke up, gasping.

That was then. This is now. And now, Davey runs for his life.

ELEVEN

One must never forget, however, that the Great Game in itself is as dangerous as the Long Game. Dreams can kill, but knives and bullets will do the job just fine as well.

— From Sir Richard Francis Burton's private journals

January wasn't expecting that. And she wasn't expecting the gun.

"Don't worry, Miss Purcell," he said. "Everything is under control."

She frowned at him. "And what makes you think that?"

"Like yourself, I also work for a higher power."

Then January remembered where she had heard of his name before.

"Moriarty."

Moran scowled.

"You've heard of my master, then," he said.

"In many of my other realities, he is nothing but a character in a book. And so are you."

"Excuse me," Dr. Jones said. Although paler than ever before and with an air of deep exhaustion, he nevertheless seemed interested in what was going on. "I must understand this right. Are you all working for different groups of dream travellers?"

"Yes," January and Sklodowska answered at the same time. Moran just nodded. Dr. Jones didn't look impressed, but curious.

"Then," he said, breathing deeply. "What do we do now?"

"Well, if this is a lucid dream," Jones said, "then we should be able to wake up at any minute and find ourselves back at the train."

"We should," said Sklodowska. "But, as Moran said, the dream is his. That means only he can wake us up. And he won't."

"Exactly, Miss Sklodowska. You see, my master had everything calculated with the utmost precision. Your group of Anarchronists established contact with the Vril-Ya, but he happened to discover another race of beings who use the dreamspace. Unfortunately, they are not able to use this method to travel between realities, so they asked him to help them come here. And he agreed."

"For a price," January said.

"Of course, madam," Moran added. "He wants to be the ruler of this world."

"So," Jones said, "Moriarty is the man who sold the world, after all."

Sklodowska shook her head fiercely. "Not if I can help it." And she turned to the door, which immediately started to shimmer and seemed to dissolve. The Vril-Ya who entered was a female.

"You do not need to tell me what is happening," she said. And, to Jones and Sklodowska: "You two, come with me. The Magistrate calls."

"The hell you'll go," Moran said, flustered. "Let's wake up, shall we?" And snapped his fingers.

Nothing happened.

He repeated the gesture. Again and again.

He looked shocked.

"You do not seem to realise," the female said, "that we of the Coming Race are mind-readers, and we can also influence lesser beings. Sleep now."

Moran collapsed, as completely as a puppet with his strings cut. From where she was, January saw that he was breathing. In fact, his countenance was that of a man sound asleep, without a care in the world.

"No more dreaming for now," the female said. "Come."

Jones and Sklodowska followed her out of the door. Before January could follow, the door reappeared, trapping her inside the building.

Then she noticed something.

Where's Hans? She looked around. The room was spacious, but not so big that the huge guide could have escaped her attention. Until she noticed a stairway in the back.

Everything seemed to be built from the same alabaster-like material, so translucent that January had to adjust her focus all the time so she wouldn't bump into things, or trip on the steps; steps that were just the right size for normal humans, she noted, which caused her to wonder if they had entertained other human visitors in the past.

Hans was waiting for her at the end of the stairs.

"I am sorry," he said, "but I decided to explore a bit on my own. I was just descending when I heard the voice of that strange woman."

"Hans, were you aware of their existence?"

The guide shook his head. "No. We never met them last time."

"Did you find something?"

"This building is just three storeys high. From it we can jump to other, smaller buildings. I noticed they are all too close to each other."

She led the way.

"Another thing," Hans said. "If what the Magistrate called the Stream is what I think it is, then we might be able to escape in a very straightforward way to the surface."

"And what it is?" she asked him.

"A river," he said. "A very big river."

"Hansbach," January said, remembering that – according to the book at least – Professor Lidenbrock and his nephew Axel named it in Hans' honour, because he had been the one who found it just when they had run out of water.

"Yes," he said. "I was happy then. I thought it was a good thing."

"And is it not?"

He shrugged. "It wasn't important. It never meant anything in my life. I continued my work as a guide, I married, had children… It is a good life, Miss Purcell, I'm not complaining. But it wasn't really important. It was like a dream, a dream that you have and then forget with the passage of time."

As are our entire lives, January thought. She was glad she could travel in dreams and escape the utter cruelty of a single reality, linear in time.

"It's my first time here since Professor Lidenbrock's expedition," he said. "I must admit I missed the excitement."

"But not that much," January countered with a tired smile. He laughed.

"No, not that much."

They had reached the top of the stairs now. January found a terrace with a balcony and a bridge of sorts, connecting this building to another, a small white ziggurat. She looked around.

"Do you see bridges in the surrounding buildings as well?"

Hans squinted.

"No."

She went around the balcony. There was no other way out but the bridge. January had a very disturbing thought involving abattoirs.

"What do you think, Hans?"

The guide pondered a bit.

"Aside from the strange entrance door down there, I couldn't find any other door that could close and block our way," he said. "If there's no escape in front of us, we can retreat and try to jump to some other building. It will be hard, but not impossible."

January wasn't that worried with having to jump. But she knew she had to see this to the end.

"Let's go then," she said.

They crossed the bridge with care, looking around, but their surroundings were empty of people. In fact, the whole town looked abandoned.

During the two minutes they took to cross the bridge, though, January was more concerned with Moran. The Vril-ya put him to sleep, but the rest of the party didn't wake up. This would require a more radical measure.

Somehow, January was expecting the ziggurat was bigger on the inside. In fact, it was much smaller, sporting only an amphitheatre very similar to the Theatre of Dionysus Eleuthereus in Athens, which she had visited with her parents in that very reality when she was twelve.

The amphitheatre was full to the brim with other Vril-Ya, all of them similar to each other, almost as if they were copies. They were in complete silence, which was disturbing.

The atmosphere was suffocating. And she hadn't even looked down yet.

Down, at the semi-circular stage in front of the steps of the theatre, stood the Magistrate, along with Dr. Jones and Sklodowska. In the centre of the stage, a silvery-white pool gleamed, hurting January's eyes. The Stream?

There was another thing in the centre. A kind of pedestal made of the same material as everything there, balancing on three legs so thin that January thought for a moment the wooden box on top of it was floating on air.

"Today we celebrate the fulfilment of our dreams," the Magistrate said in his booming voice. "The same dream the powerful Vril infused us with, allowing us to enter the Stream and other worlds via the oneiric passages, is the dream that now permits us to meet this human from the surface, with his marvellous contraption. Now we will be able to contact our brethren from across the gulf of space, who will help us to reclaim the Earth, as is our right."

Jones and Sklodowska were in thrall. They didn't seem themselves.

Then the Magistrate gestured to the couple. Sklodowska went to the fore.

"Before today," she said, "we had the means, but not the power. The Device is a dream come true, but so it is the encounter between our two worlds. By means of the Stream that the Vril-ya so generously allowed us to use with the box, we will be able to channel all the energy we need to help turn the world into a better place."

Then it was Dr. Jones' time to speak. He seemed a bit sick, but in full control of himself. *Apparently*, January thought.

"Together," he said, "we celebrate today a new pact. A pact that symbolises a new world, to be built on the ruins of the old one: a world where humans, Vril-Ya and people from other spheres can coexist peacefully and thrive."

"And now," Sklodowska said, pointing to the box which Jones was opening to reveal a huge diamond the size of his fist, "we can begin this new world."

Jones activated the mechanism. A blinding flash of light inundated the amphitheatre.

"Fuck," January said.

Interlude

Yet across the gulf of space, minds that are to our minds as ours are to those of the beasts that perish, intellects vast and cool and unsympathetic, regarded this Earth with envious eyes, and slowly and surely drew their plans against us, aided by other minds living under this Earth.

The Martians saw the signal in their dreams and out of them as well, for the shaft of pure light produced by the box was thrust into the sky like the pike of an Imperial Lancer, and reached the black of space far beyond Earth's atmosphere. It shone over the blue planet like a beacon for mariners.

Or conquerors.

So, they came to conquer.

TWELVE

Linear time is the cruellest of times.
To escape it, you must dream –
But if even the dream will not suffice
Plunge deeper into the stream.

– Unknown author

"Quick," January said, turning back to where they had come from. "We must get out of here." Her eyes hurt badly from the flash of light. She tried reaching to Hans, but she couldn't find him.

"Are you all right, Miss Purcell?" he asked, but something in his tone wasn't quite right.

"I'll be fine in a moment," she said. "The thing is, we don't have a moment. Help me, please."

"I'm afraid that will not be possible," the voice replied. Then January realised what was wrong.

It wasn't Hans's voice. The tone was raspier, older, and very bitter.

"I see you still haven't recognised me," he said, adding a layer of irritation to his voice. "When Moran was disabled, I opted for the only possible course of action. So, I had to come."

"Moriarty," she breathed.

"In flesh and blood, even if not mine own," he said, gripping her arm suddenly. "Although I wonder if the stuff of dreams is lighter. But we can certainly find that out, can't we?" And he tried to throw her off the balcony.

His grip was strong, but January was stronger; even half-blind, she could see where his face was. So, she punched him as hard as she could.

It was enough for him to release her arm. She ran back to the building as fast as she could. Hans, or Moriarty (*but how?* she wondered) – was nowhere to be seen.

She was tired and hurt, and a bit disoriented, not only because of the flash of light. Being inside a dream could do that. January was pretty pissed off with herself for having fallen so easily into such a trap. Right now, there was only one thing she could do to escape, but she would have to get rid of Moriarty somehow.

She reached the balcony of the prison building, but she didn't go for the stairs. Instead, she circled it. Her vision was returning to normal, and she could already see the surrounding buildings below.

All of them were lower, but one almost matched the height of the balcony. She could jump with reasonable certainty of success. Since she now knew this was a dream, she could try the time-honoured method of cutting lucid dreams short: plunging headfirst to the ground so she could wake up. She had done this countless times during her Oneironaut training. If that approach worked, she would probably wake up on the train to Helissandur and she would have plenty of time to convince Jones to change allegiances.

But January wasn't sure this would work in someone else's dream. So she would rather tread – or jump – lightly.

So, that's exactly what she did.

The jump was almost perfect, except for a small miscalculation regarding the volume of her winter clothes. She had to pull up her skirt before jumping, and the impact on landing unbalanced her and she twisted her left ankle. But she didn't stop because of a small sprain: limping, she searched for the stairs.

The building was fortunately empty. She descended to the ground floor, which was quite large, where she found what she was looking for. A semicircle of divans occupied one corner, designed to accommodate bodies bigger than ordinary humans. They might almost have been waiting for her.

She lay down and initiated the meditation procedure. With any luck, she would be in the House in no time.

THIRTEEN

There are many approaches to dreaming. Beyond the three usually known kinds of dream, there are plenty of levels the more experienced Oneironaut can access – provided she has the necessary training. The access to the Higher Power is one of these levels. It can be done only from inside the House, and it can be used occasionally as a means of bypassing dreams forced on the Oneironaut by others.
– From The Book of Oneiric Rules, Revised Edition

The House was in ruins.

January couldn't understand why. But she had no time to wonder. Even though the House was inside the Existing, and therefore immune to the passage of time, she couldn't risk anything happening to her body – at least not until she had attempted the Body Transfer.

The doors usually take an Oneironaut only as far as her consciousness can go. She could jump from one reality to the next, but that would solve precisely nothing. January Purcell, the part of herself that was that particular Victorian woman, would still be there, locked in the building, waiting for her fate to be decided.

The fact that she was still January Purcell was very important to her. She didn't want to jump to another time and place and forget that reality.

The only action she could take to solve this conundrum was to jump bodily. It wasn't an easy thing to do – far from it – but it was doable. She did it once in the Swinging Sixties, jumping from Tibet to Paris, in order to escape a cadre of assassins who were pursuing him up on the cold mountains. He barely escaped then. Maybe she would have a better chance now.

She looked for the stairs to the second floor. The initial flight was missing a few steps, and she had to climb very carefully, until she got to the landing.

There was only one door at the second floor.

The door to the Higher Power.

When January was first trained to be an Oneironaut, she was told that the Higher Power is not something you see in your daily life. It's more an abstract concept, actually, but an abstraction that is embodied, concretised somehow, a super-structure if you will.

Words, words, words, she thought. She had seen it with her – his – own eyes when she escaped from Tibet, and she still couldn't quite figure out what she saw. All she could tell was that it wasn't a very good feeling.

But she had no time to feel afraid. January braced herself and entered –

– into an airship. A *huge* airship: the *Heathen* was a small boat compared to this.

She was standing on a narrow walkway, but her shoes didn't make any noise, as they normally would on such a platform. She looked down. The surface appeared to be moist and fleshy, quite different from any kind of metal she had seen on other dirigibles. On the contrary: she seemed to be standing on flesh.

As if she was aboard a living ship.

She looked up. The walkway seemed infinite, and she couldn't see the other end. To her sides, the walls were translucent, except for a few, spaced portholes, which were more like puckered mouths ripped in the flesh. Beyond them, all January could see were stars.

"We are currently crossing the Dreamspace via Deneb," a feminine voice said very softly on her ear. She jumped and looked behind her, but there was no one.

January almost asked who it was, but she didn't dare to speak inside the Higher Power.

"Don't be afraid," the voice said. "You are inside me. No harm will come to you."

January wanted to say she wasn't afraid at all, but she was shivering. Even so, it was more a feeling of revulsion. She shouldn't be inside another creature. It was something she didn't expect.

"What do you require?" the voice said again.

Then January mustered the courage to talk.

"I need to be transported from inside the Earth. I am being held against my will."

"Where do you need to go?"

"Back to London. To the Oneiros Club."

A pause. January waited. She looked around, trying to get some sense of her surroundings, but she couldn't. She was freezing.

"Your timeline is under attack," the voice said again. "This was not to be. I'm afraid you won't be able to go where you want."

"So what can be done?"

Another pause. A briefer one this time.

"Go right ahead. You will be taken as close to your goal as we can muster. As soon as you get there, you will be transported."

January didn't wait.

She walked for a few minutes, then she started to get irritated. She walked faster. Around her, she could feel shapes moving, shadows in strange colours swirling in the walls, the walls themselves melting into other, weirder things. She suddenly noticed she wasn't in the interior of a ship any more, but she preferred not to pay attention to that. She had the feeling she would be safe as long as she kept walking.

Then she saw another door. It was very different from all the others in the House. It was more like a blast door, but also not made of metal.

When she got closer, January could see that the door pulsed. It was warm to the touch, and she couldn't find any kind of handle. She started to run her hand over it, and to her surprise the door purred. And irised open to her.

She crossed the threshold –

– and then, suddenly, in the ruins of London, January Purcell was running for her life.

She literally hit the ground running, in a line as straight as it could possibly be. The rubble in the street occluded the view of her surroundings for as long as her eye could see, and her eye could usually see very well and at a long distance. The mayhem brought to mind the Great Fire of 1666. Then the city had been almost completely ravaged by flames, to a point where several men who could still remember the layout of the city were hired to help ensure the streets could be restored to their original state. Now she remembered that one of her counterparts had been among that group.

But that was long ago. It was 1888, and she was alone in the ruins of a London ravaged by Martian death machines.

"Not quite alone, Miss Purcell," someone shouted to her from across a big black boulder which used to be the head of one of the Trafalgar Square lions. She stopped and turned around to see Burton walking in her direction.

"What are you doing here, Sir Richard?"

"I could ask you the same thing, Miss Purcell," he said, scowling. "If the Higher Power hadn't already told me to expect you. Come with me. We have some adjustments to make."

Interlude

David is getting closer to the hospital. He's thin, but not quite fit. He drinks and smokes a lot. David is running as if the world around him were coming to an end. But he doesn't quite know what sort of end it is.

Nevertheless, he persists. Even though he has no idea of what he's doing.

FOURTEEN

The Time Tomes – or simply the Registers – are records of activities. Originally conceived as a sort of book-keeping system to track members, it later became more sophisticated, working also as a general record of their counterparts, at least the ones who jumped to 1888, the focal point of the Oneiros Club.

— From *A History of the Oneiros Club*

January went back to the Centre of the Earth. She didn't want to think about it. But the truth is that Burton didn't have to convince her much. She asked for his help, after all; therefore, she had to listen to his advice.

But first she followed him to the Oneiros Club – or what remained of it. The building was in ruins, but Burton pointed her to an underground entrance.

The wine cellar of the club was immense. It ran the entire length of the building. Burton turned on the lamps, and January could see several long tables, full of books and maps. On a dark table in the centre of the cellar, there was a huge book.

"This," Burton started to leaf through it, "is one of the Time Tomes. This is where we register the memories of our members' travels across dimensions."

"You could have spared me a great deal of trouble if you had let me read these books in the first place," January said.

"I thought you would have realised by now that all our actions serve a purpose," he replied.

"You could have also told me that."

"If I could, I would have done so."

"Can I hear it now?"

"You are here."

"What should I do, then?"

And he told her.

So she returned. Normally she would have woken up, but in such cases the process was very straightforward. She went back to the Higher Power and took the same path as before. This time, however, the Power conducted her to a different place, where she again hit the ground running upon arrival. She had no time to lose.

She entered the Centre of the Earth in a narrow street smack in the middle of the Vril-ya city. There was no one in sight. January listened. She could hear a small murmur, and soon she saw the ziggurat blazing.

It was like a bonfire, but a sheer white bonfire confined to a straight column, which streamed out of the ziggurat by its chopped-off top and went straight to the vaulted ceiling. January had to squint to see it in all its brilliance. The light was blinding.

Only then did she notice that there was an opening right above the ziggurat. And the beam of pure light entered the hole.

Burton had told her what this was all about. But she wondered if Jones knew the truth.

It was her job to get to him and take him out of here. If possible, the others as well.

Not Sklodowska, though. She could take care of herself.

She entered the ziggurat from behind. Now the Vril-ya were streaming out of the exits, in a perfectly orderly fashion.

"Go, brethren!" the Magistrate exhorted. "Go to the surface! There we will meet our brothers from the Red Planet. They will help us scourge the world and put mankind in their proper place, serving us!"

January found Jones. He was leaning against a wall, seemingly exhausted. Sklodowska noticed her approach.

"Too late now, Oneironaut," she said. "You can't stop the inevitable."

"I know," January said, grabbing Jones' arm.

"What are you doing?" Jones asked.

"I can't explain now, sorry," January said. "Let me take you to a safe place first."

"I am afraid you will do nothing of the sort," said the Magistrate. With a gesture, he closed the doors in front of them.

January looked around. She was surrounded by Vril-ya on all sides. She turned and saw Sklodowska. She didn't look amused.

"I'm not sure why you tried to escape," she said. "You will accomplish nothing."

January bit back a curt response, biding her time.

"Our brethren from the other sphere shall arrive soon," the Magistrate said. "You will remain here. We do this to assure your safety, not because we wish you any harm."

"He speaks the truth," Sklodowska said.

"But do you?" January retorted.

"What do you mean?"

"What have you been doing with David all this time?"

"Helping him."

"By giving him poison?"

"What is going on here, by Jove?" Jones said. He was astonished.

"You are feeling more and more exhausted, isn't that so? I've been noticing it."

"I have a rather delicate constitution, I'm afraid. But I have taken my medicine for years now. Miss Sklodowska has nothing to do with that."

"But she has been dallying with you recently. I daresay your trysts have been happening since Paris, no?"

Sklodowska scoffed.

"Pierre Curie was a mediocre scientist… and lover. David is a better man in all the senses."

"Really, Marie! Now is not the proper time," Jones said.

"What of your dreams? You have been dreaming more and more vivid dreams lately, right?"

"Yes. I believe I already told you that."

"This is part of a training to become an Oneironaut."

"Are you telling me I am one of your kind?"

"Every one of us on this Earth can ride the waves of dream, my dear fellow," the Magistrate interrupted. "But only the Vril-Ya have the ability to shape them, and to communicate with other spheres beyond this."

"Do you dream of the Martians?" January asked him.

"For a long time now," the Magistrate nods.

"But is it true?" Jones asked. He seemed dizzy. "Life on Mars?"

"We felt other intelligences, other than human, around us in the ether, but we weren't quite sure where they dwelled," the Magistrate explained. "Then, one day, we discovered that the Vril – this is the name we give to the stream that crosses our domains – amplified our capacity throughout the space. And we came to meet the Martians, as you call them – but they have another name for themselves, a name that, like ours, is much too hard for mere humans to pronounce."

"And what happened then?" January asked.

"They need to find a new home, for theirs has been ravaged centuries ago. They dwell in the underground like we do."

"So, you allied with them and invited them to come," Jones ventured.

"That is correct."

"One thing I don't understand," Jones said. "What does Moriarty have to do with this scheme?"

"Elementary, my dear fellow," the Magistrate said, making January cringe. "He was the one who, how can I say this in a way you can understand... "connected the dots". He approached us a few months ago trying to strike a deal, but I'm afraid his price was too high."

"World domination," January offered.

"Precisely," said the Magistrate. "With himself seated at the throne as Ruler Absolute. We found this in very bad taste, for the Vril-ya believe firmly in democratic rule. There's no place for dictators in our new world."

"What will happen when the Martians arrive?"

"They will prepare the surface for us."

January frowned.

"How?"

"Eradicating most of the human presence there."

January whipped her head round to see Sklodowska's reaction. "Are the Anarchronists in accord with this?" she asked.

Sklodowska had gone pale. "I can't say we are. But it's too late now."

January shook her head. "No, it's not." And, taking Jones by the hand, she ran to the Stream and jumped.

Interlude

David arrives at the hospital. He stumbles his way past the ER doors. The receptionist shouts after him, but there is no one else to try to stop him. He is exhausted and feeling dizzy. Why does he remember his strange Victorian dream from earlier tonight?

In the dream, he was talking to a beautiful woman. She was blonde and very white, but she carried herself like a man (and he felt even more attracted to her for that). And she was talking to him about people who travelled in dreams. Not any travel; people who used dreams as a means of transport, just like using a train or a plane. And she was telling him two of the strangest things: first that he was one of those people, even though he couldn't remember it.

And, the most bizarre thing of all: that he knew her in 1968, and she was his friend JP. But JP was dying, and he needed help.

So he went to rescue him.

He was getting there.

FIFTEEN

As there are many Houses, one for each Oneironaut, so there are also many other symbolic systems of travelling via dreams. When the Anointed One talks about many mansions in his father's house, one wonders if he wasn't by any chance one of us. Some, however, consider this thinking heretical.

— From Sir Richard Francis Burton's private journals

The stream was cold. It was also strangely comfortable.

On impact, January had closed her eyes instinctively, but now she opened them. And what she saw was unbelievable.

They weren't in water.

They were floating in some kind of amber.

The most startling thing January saw was Jones. No, *David*: she would have to get accustomed to his change of names, but now he really seemed a completely different person. His blonde hair now looked redder in the amber, his cheeks fuller.

And he was breathing.

And talking.

"Where are we now?" he asked her. "Are we dreaming?"

Then she noticed she was also breathing.

"That seems the only rational explanation," she said. "Although we cannot tell from where we are. We don't know what kind of substance Vril is."

"Can you see if they are coming for us?"

She looked up.

"Nothing."

"Maybe we are dreaming then," he concluded. "They are very powerful with their minds. I suppose the Magistrate would have already lifted us out of the Stream purely by the power of thought by now."

"At last someone has intelligence enough to understand what's going on," said a voice behind them.

They turned and saw Burton.

They were not entrapped in amber any more. January recognised the place immediately: they were in the Higher Power. Their surroundings were far more spacious than before – instead of the quasi-infinite walkway, they were standing on a platform over a swirling multi-coloured void.

"Edgar Allan Poe and Chuang Tzu have defined with a reasonable degree of certainty the situation we find ourselves in now," he went on.

"A dream within a dream?" David asked suddenly.

Burton made an approving face. "If you will," he said. "The truth, as always, is simpler, even though more difficult to explain. We are not quite inside dreams, but navigating our way around them, linking realities and sliding through."

"This whole mechanics of dreaming is fascinating," David said. January saw that his bad eye seemed to glitter with the silvery reflection of the maelstrom below them. "If I understand correctly, dreams are not illusions, but gates to other realities, is that so?"

"Some of them, yes."

"And we all can learn how to open these gates."

"Some of us."

"Me too?"

"You've been doing that already for quite a while now," January said.

"But you've told me," David turned to her, "that you are capable of remembering your other incarnations, so to speak. Indeed, I've been having constant dreams in the same scenarios, which might be part of the same reality, but aside from that, they seem like any other dream. I feel no difference at all."

Burton nodded.

"When my role in the Long Game started, I thought pretty much the same as you do. You have just begun your training. Ordinarily, you would have time enough to study in peace and quiet before doing your first jumps. I'm afraid, however, these are not ordinary times. Come with me."

He turned to a flesh-coloured blast door, pulsing and full of bluish veins. He touched one of the veins and pinched it. January

85

could swear she heard a low-pitch shriek. The door folded open as a gaping wound. Burton stepped through and they followed suit.

Ruins everywhere. At a distance, they watched the Martian tripods sending fire and brimstone upon the streets of London.

"My God!" David said. "What scary monsters are these?" But he seemed more intrigued – and excited, thought January – than afraid.

"The Martians," Burton said. "They have, indeed, destroyed more than they were supposed to. But in the end they will be defeated by the same invisible enemy that was their undoing the last time. And the end won't be long in coming."

"The last time?" January asked.

"Part of this already happened before," Burton explained. "At least once, as Wells described. But that happened in another reality."

"Which in my counterpart's reality is just fiction," she said.

"Exactly. This one is a sort of para-reality, where many of the stories we consider fiction have really happened. It's not uncommon, actually. You should have visited a bookstore here. They have the strangest books."

"I'm not sure I want to spend more time here," she said.

"But this body…" David said, blushing as soon as he blurted the words. "I mean, your physical self, it belongs here, right? Then how can you…?"

"How can I not be here any more, you ask? I can't, David. I will still be here, always. But part of my consciousness can be projected back to where I first started my journey, and 'this body', as you so aptly put it, is not the starting point."

"What is?"

"Another time, in our future. We are friends there as well."

"In fact, that is exactly where I want to send you," Burton said.

SIXTEEN

Time runs differently in each reality. However, every time an Oneironaut jumps across realities, she creates a kind of bridge for a while, thus establishing a one-to-one correspondence. This usually makes for an easier, less confusing travelling between realities.

— From *The Book of Oneiric Rules, Revised Edition*

It was a fast, focused training; the hardest January ever remembered doing. Even in her Swinging Sixties incarnation, she had never run the gamut of dreaming to such an extent. They started with meditation and lucid dreaming, still in the realm of imagination. After that, David could dip his toes in the ocean of memory, and January started leading him into his own cache of remembrances.

"I still have a certain problem with the synchronisation," he said at the end of the first day.

"What are you experiencing?" January asked.

"A bit of a headache and double vision. As if I was intoxicated. I remember feeling like that once in Paris with…" he trailed off. "You know who. We drank absinthe in Le Chat Noir with Debussy and Toulouse-Lautrec." He sighed.

"It takes some time to adapt," January told him.

"But do we have this time?" he asked. Jones looked genuinely distressed. "I have the feeling that we are wasting time."

"Time runs differently between realities," she said. "Since you haven't synchronised with your 1968 counterpart, this difference in timing allows for a little respite. We are teaching you the basics as fast as we can."

"Will it be enough?"

"It better be," she said.

The next day, they visited the House.

It was an interesting house. Not quite hers, probably not quite his either. It was a clean, well-lit place, with ample corridors and an impressive number of huge white doors. It reminded January of a palace in Switzerland she had once visited with her parents in another reality.

"What is all this?" he asked her, looking amazed.

"This is how we enter other realities. A symbolic system which might seem a bit quaint but is very helpful nonetheless. We need concrete images to anchor our thoughts and avoid drifting away."

"Drifting where?"

She made a vague gesture. It was interesting, she noticed, how her hand seemed to create a sort of dim grey afterimage.

"All around. Across realities. It used to happen a lot in the early days. Since we created this system, however, these occurrences have become very rare."

"And each door corresponds to a reality?"

"Exactly."

"And I can access any I choose?"

"Not quite. The Higher Power has its own set of criteria; they make available only the door through which you are needed at any given moment. The others remain locked."

"Will I be able to come here on my own?"

"From now on, yes, since you know the way in. But I will be with you on our next few incursions. You need to acclimatise yourself, get the lie of the land, so to speak."

When they woke up, Burton was waiting for them. He was sitting on a chair, calmly smoking his pipe. David got up slowly, apparently dizzy, but beside himself with joy.

"This is everything I want to do now," he said, beaming. "God, I feel young again!"

Burton didn't smile. "You might go easy on that, Jones. To travel in dreams is not unlike drinking or using opium: it gives you an inebriated feeling, but there will be a price to pay later."

"I imagine that the price is high," Jones said, "but I suspect that if I could not pay it, you wouldn't have brought me here."

"That is true," January said. "But you need training."

"Speaking of which," Burton said, "I want to teach you how to prepare your mind for the jump. To steel yourself so you don't collapse under the weight of your other counterparts. Then we pay another visit to the House."

January went to the stairs. "What about her?" David asked.

"I have an errand to run," she said. "I'll be back later."

"Isn't it dangerous outside?"

"It is," she agreed, "but I'm not going outside."

January went straight to Burton's scriptorium, the only place in the club that wasn't affected by the blasts of the tripods. She lay on the tattered, dusty Shiraz rug and closed her eyes.

But sleep didn't come easily for her. According to the last reports Burton received just before the fall of London, the Martians had landed all over the UK, and also in France, Germany, Spain, and Sweden. There were far more than the ten cylinders Wells wrote about when his book was only a fiction. And they were devastating not only the countryside, but cities. Many cities. Paris had fallen. Also Berlin. Munich and Salzburg.

And now London.

Her heart was beating faster. Fortunately, though, she was also tired. She took a deep breath. Two. Three. And started to meditate.

This time the House was different. It was darker, its doors all hiding in shadow, as if dusk was falling. But there was no dusk here: on close examination, the walls were cracking; they had hairline fissures crisscrossing them all. She looked around; as far as she could see, the doors were all closed and blackened, as if covered with soot. Suddenly, she discovered she didn't know where to go, which door to access.

She chose the nearest one and tried to open it.

It wouldn't budge.

This had never happened before.

"Goin' out, are ya, Miss Purcell?"

Startled, she turned.

She didn't recognise the form in front of her – her 'eyes' are just an abstraction when in the House. Only her essence is present. But she never – in all of her versions – had to worry about it, because she had never been with a fellow Oneironaut in the same House.

So, she simply couldn't recognize who was there with her now. All she could see was a shape – the fuzzy, grey shape of a man. She would have liked to ask him who he was, but this was neither the time nor the place to do so. This wasn't a Hollywood movie.

But, even though she could not know for sure who he was, she could guess by the tone of his voice (or his ideal voice, produced by an ideal, abstract throat): Mr. Moran.

The abstract figure ran towards her.

She didn't have time to think; all she could do was get out of the way, using a savate movement her male counterpart (and another female from the nineteen-seventies) was trained in. Mr. Moran rolled and fell to the side.

JP ran.

The corridors were not particularly narrow. It was all JP could do to not tumble down. She ran past several doors, all of them black, all diseased, all of them beyond her reach. This meant she would only be able to come back via the route that had brought her here. Would that be the same to her attacker?

She didn't have time to think. She ran.

Then she reached the main corridor, and she knew what was on the end of it. The door to 1968, to her self who was – as far as she could know – recovering from surgery. The door was green.

She went straight to it. Moran wasn't far behind.

She knew she couldn't die in the House, for her body didn't exist there. Her mind created the illusion so her consciousness could remain sane. But, damn! Her abstract heart was going to burst out of her non-existent ribcage.

JP tried the handle.

The door opened.

The next thing that happened was intriguing.

Usually, a door in the House doesn't open straight to another reality. It does, however, lead to a kind of mist, a limbo, an intermediary place where one's consciousness slowly coalesces into that reality.

Not for JP, though. Not this time.

What she felt was cold. Severe cold. She could see her breath, and feel the goosebumps on her arms and neck. For a few seconds it was as if time itself had returned, along with January's body, and she could see herself wrapped in mist. No, shrouded by it. She felt as if she had died.

Had she? Had he?

Then she saw the mists part, and Moran entered. But now the body didn't belong to Moran. The man who crossed that doorway was a bit taller and thinner, with a neck thick like a bull's, close-cropped blond hair and a crooked nose. He was dressed entirely in black, and had a pistol in his hand.

He also seemed not to notice her. He was looking ahead, and January had to turn around to see what drew his attention. They were in what seemed to be a hospital room, white, clean and ill-illuminated. There was a bed at one end of the room, and on it a man, full of tubes, with a heart monitor.

The man was her male counterpart, obviously. And Moran's counterpart was going to kill him.

Then she saw a hand reaching out for her in the other side of the mist.

At the same instant, Jones entered the House again, this time with Burton. It was the same House January had entered, with the same burnt doors, and one green door at the end, wide open.

"Why couldn't January come with us?" Jones asked him.

"She was needed somewhere else," answered Burton, rushing to the green door. "Now quiet. This is going to be strange for you."

"I am ready to embrace the strange."

"Good," Burton said, pushing Jones through the door.

"Quick! This way!" Burton extended a hand. January took it.

January woke up with a devastating headache. She couldn't even remember how she returned from the House. The first thing she did was to reach out for David, but he wasn't there. She immediately turned to Burton, who was reclining in his divan, lighting his pipe. "Did it work?" she asked him.

"Beautifully," he said, smiling.

Interlude

When David reaches the second floor of the hospital, all hell breaks loose.

What is meant by hell: the instant Victorian David's consciousness falls with the weight of God's vengeance into Swinging David's brain. His body tumbles down to roll on the floor, and somehow it feels as if both selves are tumbling down one on top of the other, like two men fighting in a pub — or (the image occurs to him in a flash, he can't figure why) two dragons forming the Taoist symbol of Yin and Yang.

He is both. He is the balance. No, scratch that; he is far from being any sort of balance. He is both one and the other, forever falling, forever into each other. For a moment, everything seems to fit.

He is one. He is whole again.

And he knows so much now.

But there is barely time to act on all this knowledge suddenly acquired (no, not so suddenly; the knowledge was always there; an alchemist told him that, in another life). He must save his friend's life.

For now he knows two very important things. The first: if his friend is killed here, then January will die as well. Because the self who starts the process is also its control, and JP started all this when he jumped right before entering a coma.

The second thing is that he loves his friend. As David here and as Robert there. Both incarnations.

Knowing this, and letting go of any pretence of heroics, just focusing on the moment, he attacks the assassin.

The fight ends as quickly as it began; in one moment, David falls over the shadow — a man, but a fuzzy man, as if he shines with black light, or as if he vibrates with energy and speed that make it impossible to focus your eyes. But the shadow is tangible all right; David's blows strike him very well.

92

One thing David — this new David, who is more than the sum of his parts, the David who knows — notices is that there is another door at the other end of the room, near the bed where his friend lies still comatose. A door to the House.

And January is on the other side.

All David needs to do is force the shadow (who is this, after all? He knows a great deal but he does not know everything, alas) to the door, so he can push him through.

And that's what he does.

But the shadow clutches him with his talons and takes him along.

After that, things get hectic.

David enters the House in his body. Something that should be impossible.

Then Burton points him to another door. "Go, quickly! You won't be able to return through the first door! Don't stop!"

He runs until the end of the corridor and opens the other door.

And everything changes one more time.

SEVENTEEN

How not to collapse
Under the weight of many selves:
Let go of you.

— Attributed to Bashô (apocryphal)

For one strange moment, that seems to last hours, David Jones is three.

The first opens his eyes on the cellar of the Oneiros Club. Burton is smoking his pipe as if he did not have a care in the world.

The second is running in the House, where January is holding Mr. Moran.

The third is standing on the surface of a red desert.

He is at the same time another incarnation and, somehow, an amalgam of the first two (and of more, unknown selves, this much he senses). His blonde hair is now red, but how does he know it, since there is no mirror there? In fact, there is nothing there but himself, dressed in a strange outfit that covers his entire body.

There is something distant but approaching fast.

In a few minutes, he can see what it is.

Giant glass spiders.

Two days later, a soldier appeared at the cellar, with a cable for Burton.

"As foreseen, the Martians succumbed to Earth's germs," he said. "His Majesty's Army is collecting the bodies and the machines of the extraterrestrials in order to study them. If a second wave arrives, we will be ready to defeat it on the ground."

"And in other terrains?" asked January.

"We have an agent in place to stop the next wave before it starts."

"Who is this agent?" a dizzy David asked, sitting in a chair. But he already knows his identity.

"You must rest," January said. "In time, you will learn more about counterparts."

"But is he truly me? I still can't quite understand how this is possible."

"What do you see now?" Burton asked.

"With my eyes open, I see this," he gestured around. "You both. But, when I close them, I see another place. As vivid as a lucid dream. Even more so. I see a red desert and strange creatures. And I see someone who is very different from me and yet is me at the same time. Is he there now?"

"Yes. He is there now. He is you. And he is he. He always was there somehow, and he has always lived there among the stars. Don't try to understand it now. In time, you will."

"But the important thing is that you fulfilled your role," January said. "When I first came here, I wasn't sure what I had to do. I didn't know where, or why. But you shone as brightly as a star. You had this black aura around you."

"A blackguard," David said half-jokingly.

"I thought of something more... cosmic," she said. "A black star, maybe."

"The colour of the aura notwithstanding," said Burton, puffing out smoke from his pipe, "the fact remains that you are now one of us."

"And what are you? What are the oneironauts?"

Burton shrugged his shoulders.

"Whatever we need to be," he said. "to help humanity."

EPILOGUE

The Martian sands are hot, but David doesn't feel it. His special suit keeps him protected from the elements.

He is not the man he was on Earth. Strangely enough, he remembers everything from his former life. David can also remember many other lives.

David. Robert. Mr. Jones. Dr. Jones. And many other pseudonyms, both male and female. It's quite interesting, actually. He wishes he could explore them all again, with the deeper understanding that knowledge can bring.

Unfortunately, this whole trip will have to wait. He is busy now, incredibly busy.

In the distance, the glass spiders approach. The automatons, piloted by the Martian intelligences, are gathering to destroy him so they can try another invasion of Earth.

He grins.

As January told him – as if she had to convince him! – he could be a hero. Not just for one day, but forever.

He braces himself and waits for the spiders.

He is having the time of his life. In *all* possible times.

SECOND EPILOGUE

In the cellar of the Oneiros Club, Burton lights a cigar and ponders.

Everything ran according to plan. Well, almost everything.

But they were still in the Long Game.

As were the Martians. And the Vril-Ya.

The Martians were taken care of, at least for the time being. Burton and January made sure that Earth would have a new guardian.

As for the so-called 'Coming Race' – what a joke! Quite unfunny, actually: they could very well come. Burton is certain that humanity will prevail in the end. They have the Higher Power on their side, and, as far as he knows, they are human. Or, at the very least, friends of the human race.

He pours a good dose of arak into a whisky tumbler, having no shot glasses left in the ruins of the club, and knocks it back. The anise tastes bitter on his tongue.

Let them come, he thinks. *We will be waiting. In their dreams.*

ACKNOWLEDGEMENTS

Thank you to Ian Whates, for the invitation to write for NewCon Press. It's a pleasure and an honour to be here, among so many writers I love. Thanks also to another Ian, Ian Watson, and Cristina Macia, for the encouragement and good advice (and an awesome time eating and chatting in cafés and restaurants in Porto).

Also to Jean-Louis Trudel, José Baltazar Pereira Júnior and Pedro Fortunato for pointing me to a good bibliography on time travel induced by dreams.

And, last but *never* least, to my wife Patricia and my stepdaughter Larissa, the lights of my life, who give me all the love I could possibly dream of.

Also from NewCon Press

Steampunk International edited by Ian Whates
English language edition of an anthology showcasing the very best Steampunk stories from three different countries: UK, Finland, and Italy; released by three different publishers in three different languages. UK contributors are George Mann (an original Newbury and Hobbes tale), Jonathan Green, Derry O'Dowd.

Night, Rain, and Neon edited by Michael Cobley
All new cyberpunk stories from Ian McDonald, Louise Carey, Jon Courtenay Grimwood, Justina Robson, Simon Morden, Gary Gibson, DA Xiaolin Spires, Al Robertson, Keith Brooke & Eric Brown, T.R. Napper, Jeremy Szal, Gavin Smith, Tim Maughan, Stewart Hotston and more.

Queen of Clouds – Neil Williamson
Wooden automata, sentient weather, talking cats, compellant inks and a host of vividly realised characters provide the backdrop to this rich dark fantasy, as stranger in the city Billy Braid becomes embroiled in Machiavellian politics and deadly intrigue.

Saving Shadows – Eugen Bacon
Award nominated collection of prose poetry and speculative micro-lit pieces by author Eugen Bacon. Complementing the written word are a series of full page illustrations by artist **Elena Betti**; thirty-five stunning images that enhance the reading experience.

The Queen of Summer's Twilight – Charles Vess
A mysterious man on a black motorbike rescues a rebellious teen from the streets of Inverness, setting in motion a series of events that will see contemporary Scotland clash with the realm of fairy, in this stunning tale inspired by the ballad of Tam Lyn.